FALL

Timothy Hargreaves

Willows West

ISBN: 979-8-99986595-5-5

For my parents

CHAPTER ONE

THE FERRY'S SIREN BLASTED LOUD AND LONG. One last call before lines were pulled and thrusters boosted the ship away from the dock.

Harald stood watching, feeling the hairs on his arm, on the back of his neck rise—emotion catching him off guard, unwelcome. He raised a hand, not to anyone in particular. Along the railing stood the men and women whose last-minute choice to leave still surprised him. Some had been counted on to contribute. Yet here they were, vanishing into an unknown no less bleak than the future they were leaving behind.

Harald turned away from the dock and lifted his gaze back toward the town—what remained there. Homes and shops stood boarded, plywood holding back a slow collapse already in motion. The streets were overgrown, pavement cracked and lifted at the edges. But higher, above the rooftops, the windmill still turned, and the sharp glint of sunlight off the solar panels offered a flicker of hope. Doom, it seemed, was still a heartbeat away.

His father was already approaching—jaw set, back straight, eyes fixed ahead. He had no interest in the ferry, or those abandoning the fragile community that remained. Harald knew what came next: the never-ending tasks that filled their days, the routines that kept the remaining few fed and sheltered, that gave shape to their decision to stay—and fight.

"Harald, head over to the radio room and give Sarah a break, will you," his father instructed. The words weren't unkind—just succinct and clear, the way directions to a fifteen-year-old son had become. There was no room for questions, and none expected.

He nodded once, just enough for his father to see. He paused, a question rising but not reaching his lips: would there ever be another boat? Was this—what was left—all there would ever be? But he let it pass and turned toward the communications center. If Sarah had spoken to the ferry captain, he might learn something new.

Harald gripped the Radio Room handle and shoved with his shoulder—entry always took both. The room was concrete, windowless, a bunker built for security—or the illusion of it. It felt like the last place that would fall, if things ever came to that. The door was sturdy, but no match for determination.

Sarah looked up as Harald entered, but kept scanning the shortwave channels, headphones still draped around her neck.

"My dad said you should take a break," he said. "I can cover the radio for a while."

She nodded, starting to rise, but before she could stand, Harald added, "Did you get a chance to talk with the ferry captain?"

A faint voice crackled from the speaker—sharp at first, then dissolving into static. Male, maybe. Foreign. A few syllables, chopped and drifting.

Sarah paused, listening. The sound faded.

"That one's been bouncing around all morning," she said quietly.

She set the headphones down gently. "And yes—I caught the captain just before they left range."

She pulled a folded slip of paper from the back pocket of her jacket and handed it to him.

"You can give this to your dad when you see him." She hesitated. "I didn't get much, but I don't think we'll be seeing another ferry."

Harald looked at her, but she kept her eyes on the radio.

"The captain said they've cut diesel allotments for runs like this. He was told just to pick up anyone who wanted out."

She gave a dry little laugh—no humor in it. "He gets paid per head. I guess they need people on the mainland... same way we need them here."

Sarah moved toward the door. "I won't be long. Keep scanning the usual range, write down anything you hear."

She paused with her hand on the frame. "When I get back, take one of the two-ways and head up to Highpoint. Check in with the families."

Harald slid into the chair Sarah had just vacated. It creaked beneath his weight—old wood, older than him, and polished smooth from years of use. He leaned forward, elbows on the desk, eyes sweeping over the shortwave rig.

The transceiver was a matte black Icom box, military surplus, scarred with nicks and dull around the knobs. A hand-labeled sticker across the top read "HF 3-30 MHz – DO NOT TOUCH SETTINGS." Below it, a tangle of coax cables fed out to the antenna mast bolted into the concrete roof above.

The unit could scan across thousands of miles—skip signals off the ionosphere, pull in voices from places no one had heard from in months. On a good day, they might catch a signal from somewhere in the Rockies—crackled voices from an inland ridge, half a continent away.

But there were limits. Too much cloud cover, wrong time of day, sunspot interference—and the silence could stretch for hours. Sometimes it was hard to tell whether the quiet meant no one was broadcasting, or nobody on the other end thought it mattered anymore.

Harald adjusted the gain dial gently. The radio hissed back at him, steady and faint—like a breath through dry grass. He picked up the notepad Sarah had left beside the rig and laid it flat in front of him. Four columns. Date, time, frequency, content. Space at the bottom for comments. He flipped back a page or two. Mostly silence. Some half-words. Static.

On a shelf above the desk, a battered Grundig transistor sat humming softly, already tuned to a frequency Sarah had set. Harald reached for it, adjusted the volume just enough to separate the voice from the static.

"...coordinated deployment of mobile units to the Queensland interior... two towns fully evacuated, others under watch. Relief vessels are being routed north from Brisbane as weather permits..."

The clipped, careful accent of the BBC World Service filtered through—calm as ever, even while describing another disaster on the far side of the planet.

Australia.

Not a war zone. Just a place too big to help all at once.

Harald listened for a while until Sarah returned. He didn't write anything down. This wasn't the kind of message you logged. Just something to carry.

The hike up the caldera to Highpoint followed a well-used trail, winding through sparse ground cover that thickened into forest as Harald climbed. The route stretched just over a mile, with nearly a thousand feet of vertical gain.

He toggled through the two-way's channels as his feet carried him uphill, walking with an easy rhythm, his gaze focused ahead of him on the trail. He thought of the summit where he'd have the view—and the line of sight—needed for solid radio calls.

The air was crisp. From the top, he'd see the surrounding islands of the archipelago laid out around him. And if the haze stayed thin, he might even glimpse the mainland—though the two-way wouldn't reach that far.

Harald reached the summit and paused, taking in the familiar view. High above, a bald eagle lazily circled, catching updrafts making flight effortless. It looked like freedom.

A dark blur on the eastern horizon—the mainland.

To the west, two uninhabited islands, difficult to reach in anything but the fairest weather. To the north, Nameth.

Smoke rose from the neighbor—chimney smoke, nothing alarming.

Harald unscrewed the lid of his water bottle and drank deeply, catching his breath after the climb.

He opened the sealed ammo box that protected the antenna connection and plugged in the radio. The short mast rose from the summit rock, its guy wires anchored to nearby trees. This setup gave him reach—better than any handheld could manage alone.

Harald pulled the weathered notebook from his pack and flipped to the page marked WELLNESS – HIGHPOINT. A few lines were already penciled in— dates, times, the names of families, a column for responses.

He glanced at the sun, just past its highest point, and nodded to himself. Midday. The usual time. Most of the families would be listening.

He keyed the mic and spoke clearly into the two-way.

"This is Highpoint check-in, Channel Nine. Calling for wellness. Anyone listening, come back with your call-sign and status."

A burst of static. Then a voice came through, steady and male.

"Nine Echo. All clear. Supplies good. The lambs are coming along."

Harald logged the entry. The family at Nine Echo always kept sheep—meat, wool, milk when they had the energy for it.

A moment later, another reply—female, older. Her voice carried calm like something practiced.

"Ridge Two. Wellness good. Garden starting to turn. Beans, mostly. Out."

He made a note of that too, glancing toward the northern slope where Ridge Two sat—half-visible between trees. Two's garden always came early, even when the rains were late.

The replies came. A dozen families living remote from town, either by their choice or because the community needed people who could grow the land.

No reply from South Hollow. Not unusual—they worked the steep plots, and mid-day often meant tools in hand, not radios.

A faint voice buzzed in next—too broken to catch. Harald marked it in the margin: "Signal on 9. Unreadable. Possibly West Ridge."

Another attempt drifted in a minute later. Just a call sign fragment. Then silence again.

He checked the page. Twelve call signs listed. nine confirmed, two unclear, one absent.

Then silence. Longer than usual. Harald was about to close the log when a sharp, girl's voice came through:

"Unicorn Six, loud and proud."

He stared at the radio.

A second passed. Two.

"...Repeat transmission?" he said, unsure if he'd misheard.

A crackle of laughter, then:

"Just messing with you. Unicorn Six checking in. All good here. Don't get all crazy about it."

Harald blinked, unsure whether to log it or ignore it. He settled on underlining the time and writing 'Unicorn Six - status OK?' with a question mark in the margin.

Harald packed up the comms equipment, neatly organized—just as he'd found it.

Turning back to the path and beginning his descent into town, he shook his head.

He knew all the families in the outlying parts of Talem. Unicorn Six could only have come from one place.

Apparently, radio protocol got a slightly more relaxed treatment on Nameth.

Lina was going through a crate outside the meeting hall as Harald approached the town, sorting through a mess of tools and assorted junk with her usual focus.

"They left a spade set," she said without looking up. "And seed trays. Why would they leave those?"

Harald gave a non-committal shrug. "Maybe they didn't have room?"

She looked up. "Or maybe they knew they weren't planting anything where they were going—back to civilization."

"Could've just been out of space," he said again.

Lina frowned. "You make room for the stuff that grows food."

He didn't argue.

"Did you know they were leaving?" she asked.

"Only when I saw them on the ferry," he said. "Same as you."

Lina seemed to accept that. She nudged the crate with her foot and stood.

"Let's head in," suggested Harald, "the meeting will be starting soon. You save me a seat. I've got to give Dad a note from Sarah."

Harald pushed open the doors to the Hall, which doubled as a schoolhouse and community dining room. Inside, about fifty people clustered in small groups, the hum of conversation tight with anticipation.

He spotted his father near the front—arms folded, speaking in a low voice to Grace. Erik's gaze moved steadily across the room, scanning the faces, weighing the mood.

When Erik saw him, he gave a small nod, motioning for him to come forward.

"I have a note from Sarah," Harald said quietly, not wanting to draw attention. He reached into his pocket and pulled out the folded paper, soft at the creases from the walk.

Erik opened it and read. His expression didn't change, but Harald saw the ripple of tension move through his jaw. He read it again, slower this time, letting the words settle.

"People need to hear this. The actual words."

Then Erik's voice shifted, softened slightly. "Go sit with Lina. We'll get started."

Lina motioned to Harald, urging him to hurry as he slipped into the seat beside her. At the front, Grace's measured voice carried across the room.

"Let the record note," she began, "the people of Talem held a meeting this tenth day of July. Our first order of business, as always, is to report on the health of our community."

There was a flicker of hesitation—glances traded across the room. Some clearly felt that ferry news should take precedence. But order held.

Callum stood first. "We've added significant goods to inventory since the last meeting. Everything's catalogued, and several items are ready for repurposing."

Peter rose next. "Nothing to report on security. No breaks in curfew, and our blackout is holding—full compliance from dusk through dawn."

Then Sarah stood. Her tone was steady, but her eyes found Erik before she spoke. "We've had sporadic contact via shortwave since the last meeting. People out there are... unsettled. I also spoke with the ferry captain over UHF while he was at the dock."

Callum stood again, voice louder now, cutting across the room. "What the hell is going on, Erik? Why were three families allowed to leave? We're down to fewer than a hundred souls. I'd say we're inching closer to failure every day."

He paused, letting the weight of it settle before driving the point home.

"Once the batteries go, we're back in the Stone Age."

Harald noted—as usual—that Callum was the loudest voice in the room. He glanced at his father, who had remained silent until now.

Erik slowly reached into his jacket and pulled out the folded note. His movements were deliberate, his voice even.

"Sarah transcribed this from her conversation with the ferry captain," he said. "I'm going to read it exactly as written."

He unfolded the paper and read:

"This is the last crossing. No fuel, no crew. All mainland assets are redirected.

You are on your own. I'm sorry. Good luck to you all."

The words hung in the room for a moment, weightless and heavy all at once.

The room didn't erupt.

But Harald heard the same phrase, passed in low voices around the hall like a current: *We're on our own.*

It didn't matter that the ferry hadn't brought supplies in months. The finality of the words had landed. No one had missed it.

It was Callum who broke the silence.

"But Erik," he said, frustration creeping back into his voice, "why did they leave? Maybe things are getting better on the mainland."

Erik waited for the room to settle before he spoke. He didn't look directly at Callum, but his words answered the question.

"We can't know for sure what's happening on the mainland. Each of us carries our own version of what's gone on there—and our own ideas about what's coming."

He paused, letting that truth breathe.

"But what we do know is this: our community—this island—still has the resources to support us. It's a simple life. But if we choose to, we can make it a fulfilling one."

His gaze swept the room now, steady but not confrontational.

"The families who left... that was their choice. I wouldn't have made it."

Harald said nothing. Around him, the room seemed to settle into a deeper stillness—not agreement, but something close to acceptance. He glanced at the note again, now folded on the table beside his father's hand.

We're on our own.

It wasn't news. But now it was real.

Chapter Two

IT WAS A STUDY DAY, but the space still carried the echo of last night's meeting, like the room wasn't quite ready to let go of words spoken.

Harald's arms were full of things no longer needed. Three sweaters, a pair of curtain panels, and a seat cushion faded at the edges. Not broken. Just left behind.

Study days always began with repurposing. Grace said it helped people focus—hands first, then minds. Today, the leftovers from the departing families would be added to the community's growing inventory: not of things, but of *materials*. Thread, cloth, stuffing. What could be taken apart and used again.

He set the bundle down on the sorting table, unwrapped it carefully.

Nothing wasted. That was the rule now.

The room began to fill. First came the island's children. Then the adults—always welcome at study. They sat side by side and began the familiar work: picking at stitching, winding back wool. Deconstructing, but still creating—raw materials to be used again.

After a while, the groups set aside their tasks and drifted into the workshop. The nuts and bolts of the island—this place of making and mending—held a kind of reverence for Harald.

The smell was hard to pin down: the sweetness of lubricating oil, the bite of iron filings, and the warm incense of pine shavings. Morning light angled through the windows, catching on coils of salvaged copper and the smooth, pale faces of planed boards stacked along the back wall.

Cari was already there, sleeves rolled up, a small circle of students gathered loosely around her—some seated on overturned crates, one older woman on a folding stool she'd brought herself.

In her hand, she held a pellet the size of a thumb knuckle—brown, compacted, pocked like bread dough.

"This one's just sawdust and binder. Mostly fir shavings," she said, passing it around. "The heat comes from the density. Not as clean as ethanol, but it burns steady. Great for cabin stoves, now that the propane's mostly gone."

A few murmurs of interest. An adult nodded thoughtfully. A boy of about ten lifted the pellet to his nose and sniffed.

On the workbench behind Harald sat the opened shell of an old electric motor. He tapped it with a screwdriver.

"This came out of a treadmill," he said. "The belt was shot, but the rotor's still sound. I'm trying to fix it up—see if it can hold torque. If it does, we'll add it to working inventory."

One of the youngsters fixed Harald with a stern look.

"Why can't you just fix the treadmill?"

Harald paused, a hint of a smile tugging at one corner of his mouth.

"Jake, if you need exercise, you can hike up to Highpoint. There's plenty of places to walk around here without going nowhere."

Grace entered without announcing herself. She always moved quietly. This morning she wore her worn blue cardigan, the elbows patched in waxed linen, her long grey hair bound back in a single plait. She nodded at Harald and took her place near the wall.

"All right," she said. "Let's talk about the kings."

Grace didn't care where the lessons happened. The workshop was as good as the study hall.

The room stilled. A few more trickled in—an older man with dark-rimmed glasses, a young mother with a child balanced on her hip. Someone handed Grace a warm mug.

"There were three of them," she began. "Not kings by birth. Not even kings in the old way. But they carried the authority of empires. This was after a terrible war—one that scarred continents and burned cities from the air. The world was broken. So the kings met, at a place called Yalta, to divide what was left and decide how it would be ruled."

She glanced at the motor on the bench.

"One held the west. One held the east. And one—the third—wanted to build something new from the ashes.

Together, they made a kind of peace. Not a perfect one. But it lasted. Trade routes reopened. Factories retooled. The world began to spin again—faster than ever."

Harald leaned against the wall, arms crossed, listening.

"People called it a golden era," Grace went on. "You could get strawberries in winter. Satellites stitched the sky. But there was a cost. The kings had planted the seeds of empire. Everything became connected—and fragile. When the ice melted and the markets buckled, when the rivers dried and the fires raged, fuel ran thin... the threads that held it together strained. Some of them snapped."

For a moment, no one spoke.

Then the man with the glasses shifted in his seat. His voice was quiet, edged with something—nostalgia, or maybe just fatigue.

"I still don't see why it had to end," he said. "If they'd done things differently. Less greed, more foresight. We had so much."

Grace gave a small nod but didn't speak.

Harald did.

"What about now?" he asked. "What will happen to the world?"

The question lingered.

Callum leaned forward, arms braced on his knees. His voice, loud and forceful last night, carried something different now.

"Same thing that always happens," he said. "Some parts'll break. A lot of people'll get hurt. Some won't. And the rest of us—here on Talem—we'll keep going. I'm guessing it won't be as easy as we'd like."

He didn't say it unkindly. Just plainly. Like it was the only answer worth giving.

Grace had watched the exchange with a look of quiet satisfaction, like she seemed to enjoy watching others work things through as much as sharing her own thoughts. "Let's remember," she murmured. "History teaches us nothing lasts forever. Change—growth, decay, rebuilding—that's the rhythm of the world. Long before us. Before the dinosaurs. Before anything with breath or roots."

She glanced around the workshop, the copper coils, the salvaged wood, the half-rebuilt motor.

"Live in this moment," she said. "It has its rewards."

Grace's words settled over the group, taking root. For a moment, no one moved.

Then Harald stepped toward one of the workbenches, lifting a small tin in his hand.

"This is the latest batch," he said, opening the lid to reveal a neat row of pellets, each pressed and cooled in the molds he'd made himself. "They're solid. Should hold shape better than the last batch."

A few of the older kids perked up. One of the adults raised an eyebrow.

"If anyone wants to practice with the air rifles," Harald asked, "we'll set up targets out back."

There was a rustle of movement—some stretching, a few quiet voices. A pair of boys stood and headed toward the door. Cari gave Harald a small nod and began gathering a handful of folded rags to use as backstops.

The workshop began to empty—not in a rush, but with a sense of quiet purpose. Grace stayed where she was, sipping her mug, watching.

Outside, the morning had sharpened—cooler air, the smell of earth lifting off the grass. The scratch of boots on the porch. The clink of tin against a belt.

Shooting practice wasn't just for sport anymore. On Talem, everything had a reason.

CHAPTER THREE

HARALD STOOD HARD on the pedals. The old cruiser bike was heavy and slow to get going, but once it picked up speed, the effort lessened and he settled into the deep, worn seat. Before the collapse—when the island had drawn summer tourists—these bikes plied the coastal roads, their riders savoring the leisurely pace and ocean views.

Harald's view was not theirs.

The road had narrowed, hemmed in by alder and bramble as nature pressed in from both sides. Even the asphalt was vanishing—pushed aside by frost, broken open by roots, resisting nature's insistent demand but losing ground all the same. Still, the bicycle was the most efficient way to reach the far side of the island.

The saddle was cracked and sun-faded, the handlebars marked with rust, but the bike itself moved quiet and sure. Harald had tuned every bearing, tensioned the chain, adjusted the brakes. It rolled smooth—efficient and almost elegant in its purpose. What mattered to Harald was not how it looked, but how it worked.

Harald's first stop came quickly—the Gaithers' place. Tidy, well-kept, and clearly still a working holding. He dropped off the minutes from the last town meeting, notes taken by Grace and transcribed by Sarah for delivery to the dozen scattered homesteads.

Efficient communication was dear to his father's heart.

The Gaithers were friendly, asking after the meeting and those who'd left the island. Harald told them what little he knew, then jumped back onto the bike and headed off toward his next drop.

He made a couple more stops, handing off minutes and brief updates, before reaching the last name on his list: the Harrisons' place, near the end of the west road—the last inhabited property before the old mansion.

Beyond it, the land rose into shadow. Wren Grove. Old trees, old house.

Harald thought he might take a look once his deliveries were done.

He coasted to a stop just past the gatepost, where a sun-faded wooden sign warned that visitors ought to have a good reason for disturbing Reid and Marla. It looked more run-down than he remembered.

He dismounted and leaned the bike against a young fir that had grown up where the fence line used to be kept clear.

In the distance, a sloped patchwork of garden caught the light—makeshift irrigation lines glinting among rows of late-season vegetables. Whatever else had gone slack, the farmwork was clearly in hand.

Marla met him halfway up the path, wiping her hands on a flour-dusted apron.

"Minutes from the meeting," Harald said, pulling the folded packet from a zippered bag.

She took them with a grateful nod. "Good timing. Reid's anxious to hear what was said."

From inside came the unmistakable sound of Reid muttering, followed by the sharp clatter of metal on wood.

Marla sighed. "Come on, Harald. Let's go see what the old fool's up to now."

Harald followed her up onto the shaded porch and ducked through a low doorway.

Reid was hunched over the kitchen table, scowling into the disassembled guts of a cracked lantern. The parts were spread across the table—gears, wires, the cloudy plastic dome—none of it organized.

"Reid, here's Harald," Marla said. "He's brought the meeting minutes—and says if you need another pair of hands for that lantern, he's willing."

She shot Harald a sideways glance, punctuated with a quick wink to make sure he caught it.

"Didn't ask for a mechanic," Reid muttered, but he shifted aside to make room.

Harald stepped in, bent over the table, and took a quick look. The problem was clear: the rotor's contact was oxidized and the spring behind it had slipped off its catch.

He popped it back in place, rubbed the contact clean with the edge of his shirt, and gave the crank a spin.

The LED flickered—then held steady.

"Old contacts," Harald mumbled. "If you spin them periodically it'll keep the connections from seizing."

Reid issued a grunt that Harald took to be vaguely approving. The old man picked up the lantern, gave it a spin himself, and set it on the shelf.

"While you're in a fixing mood," Reid said, gesturing out the back window, "the water pump float's acting up again. Either it won't shut off, or it won't turn on. You'd think by now we'd have something better than a toilet flapper running the damn thing."

Harald followed him outside and down to the edge of the garden, where the gravity-fed irrigation line traced back to a small tank on the hill. The float switch was sun-bleached and half-buried in a tangle of weeds and sunflower stalks.

Harald crouched and brushed the dirt from the plastic housing. "Got any spare wire?" he asked.

The insulation on the existing line was cracked, brittle with age. He could see that with a clean rewire, the sensor would close properly again.

Ten minutes later, when Marla turned the valve at the tank, the pump engaged, hummed for a few seconds, then cut off cleanly as the float rose.

Reid stood nearby with his arms crossed. After a beat, he grunted.

"Harald, let's go get some tea," he said. "While I think on what else is broke around this place."

Harald followed him inside, feeling more at home here than he expected—and more curious than ever about the place up the road.

Inside the farmhouse, Marla poured tea from a porcelain teapot and passed Harald a thick slice of bread, still warm from the oven. The kitchen was rich with the scent of baking, as if something good was always just about to be served.

Harald took a bite. Nutty, a little sweet. He leaned back in the old ladder-back chair and nodded approvingly.

The farmhouse felt good—familiar. Worn in all the right places.

Reid stirred honey into his tea with the handle of a spoon and gave Harald a quizzical look.

"So, what've you been fixing around town lately?"

Harald paused, wondering for a second if Reid was after something deeper than the question suggested. He decided probably not.

"Not much. Been forging a bunch of rifle pellets. We've been working on our marksmanship. Should help bring in more small game."

He looked down at his lap, then back at Reid.

"Reid... what do you know about the old mansion?"

"Wren House," Reid said. "Been empty near fifty years. The family lost their money long before the rest of us. Ran a big timber outfit—on the islands, the mainland too—until the business dried up."

Harald nodded slowly. "Is it true about the trees?"

"Sitka spruce and Douglas fir," Marla chimed in. "Old growth. Some over two hundred feet tall. There's even a rumor they planted a redwood somewhere on the property."

She shook her head. "Kind of ironic, really—timber barons leaving their mansion surrounded by what they didn't cut. But I guess nothing surprises anymore."

She leaned forward slightly. "I wouldn't get any ideas about treasure hunts, Harald. The roof's coming in. That place is dangerous."

Reid gave him a sideways nudge. "Got stripped years ago. Your dad pulled the old shortwave out of a back room. Rest of it either got hauled off or rotted where it sat. Rain and weather took care of the rest."

Marla clapped her hands lightly. "Enough of that. What *we* need is help with the apple harvest. How about you and that sister of yours come up for a couple of days next week? We pay in cider and pie."

Harald grinned, already imagining the taste of apple pie. "I'll check with my dad and ask Lina—but I'm pretty sure you've got a deal."

Harald thanked them for the tea and stepped out into the cooling afternoon. He checked the sun—still high enough to give him an hour, maybe more, before he needed to start back.

Instead of heading home, he turned uphill toward Wren Grove.

The house wasn't far. He'd seen it from a distance before, just shapes through the trees—but he'd never gone close.

Now seemed like the right time.

The mansion stood proud.

Old bones that spoke of permanence.

But as Harald approached, the damage became clearer—both natural and not. Just as Marla had said, the roof had folded in, sagging into the upper story. Windows were cracked, some smashed outright—likely from years ago, back when people still broke things instead of preserving them.

He paused at the threshold, then stepped inside cautiously, sticking close to the outer walls, where the structure seemed most sound.

Reid and Marla had been right.

There was nothing left here.

An old sofa slumped in the corner, more part of the forest now—brown, wet, and soft with rot. A collapsed table. A few broken chairs. The air inside was thick with damp and mildew.

Harald didn't linger.

On his way in, he'd spotted a low outbuilding tucked behind the mansion, half-swallowed by vine and undergrowth.

He felt a quiet pull in that direction. Toward the part of the estate where work had happened—where something useful might still remain.

The door to the workshop was half-swallowed by brambles. Tight, thorny growth clawed at Harald's hands and arms as he cleared a way through.

It took longer than he'd hoped, but eventually he got inside.

The roof, still intact, had preserved the interior far better than the grand house just behind it. A sagging workbench ran along one wall. Shelves lined with jars—clouded with dust but still upright. The floor was dirty, scattered with leaves and old sawdust, but mostly clear.

Harald stood, not moving, letting the space settle around him.

He wondered who had worked here. What they were like.

And what it had felt like—when the Wren family finally walked away.

Moving slowly through the space, Harald scanned the shelves, the corners, beneath the sagging workbench. Most of it was rusted or half-rotted—old tools, cracked leather gloves, a coil of wire gone green with age.

Near the back of the room, something gave him pause. A section of wall that didn't look quite right—slightly recessed, the grain of the boards off just enough to notice.

He crouched and reached into the cavity, feeling more than seeing. His hand brushed something solid. Metal. Then wood.

He pulled it free—and let out the breath he hadn't realized he was holding.

A rifle. Gas-powered. An air rifle, older but well made. The lines of the design were clean, almost elegant. Classic.

Harald stepped back and set the rifle on the bench. Then he reached into the cavity again, fingers brushing against more wood and cold metal—another weapon.

Deeper down, his hand closed on a box.

He pulled the second gun free: a shotgun. Long-barreled, the metal dark but intact.

Then came the box.

Shotgun shells. Live rounds.

Taboo.

He stood still for a moment, listening—though for what, he wasn't sure.

Carefully, he returned the shotgun to its place, then the box of shells. He checked the cavity, smoothed the tarp, making sure nothing looked disturbed.

Then he picked up the air rifle and stepped outside.

The air was cool against his face. He breathed deeply.

He just needed a little time to think.

Grabbing the bike, he wheeled it around the far side of the outbuilding, avoiding a snarl of thorns. His mind was still clouded by the find inside when something caught his eye—a glint near the creek.

He paused. Stepped closer.

Definitely man-made.

A slotted grate, just visible where the stream curved around a thicket. Outflow pipe. The rim braced with concrete—cracked, but still holding.

Harald crouched beside it and pulled his notebook from his jacket pocket.

He began to sketch, carefully noting the placement, the angles, the erosion. His father would want details. This was the kind of thing worth getting right.

Marla had told him, *"no treasure hunts."*

But Harald had the sense he might have just struck gold. This wasn't what he'd come for—maybe it was better.

CHAPTER FOUR

HARALD ROSE EARLY next day. He'd shown his father the rifle and his sketches before going to bed, but he knew his father would want time to sleep on it.

Erik's hand rested on the worn handle of the kettle, steam just starting to curl from the spout. With his other hand, he nudged the enamel pan where three eggs were just beginning to simmer. A loaf of rye sat on the cutting board beside a small pot of coulee—blackberries, by the look of it—thick and dark.

"Grab some of that bread," his father said, motioning with his chin. "It's still warm. Eggs'll be ready in a few."

Harald pulled out a chair and sat, slicing a slab from the crusty loaf.

"That rifle," Erik said, wasting no time. "It's something special."

He turned slightly toward the table, voice even but intent.

"Theoben. A Rapid 7. British company—very sought after, back in the day. It's a real weapon, Harald. More power than any of the practice pellet guns you and the others have been using."

Harald had known the gun was different. The bore— .22. Gas-powered, which meant higher velocity than the spring rifles he was used to. But it was old, and if the gas cylinder had lost pressure, it might be useless.

"I'm going to strip it down this morning," he said. "Clean it up, see what kind of shape it's really in."

"That's a good idea," Erik nodded. "Let me know what you find."

He paused, then looked directly at Harald.

"But you know what you really found out there?"

Erik took the kettle off the heat, poured the water into two mugs, then set the eggs aside to cool.

"That stream—the outflow you sketched. It's hydro," he said. "There's a turbine up there we could relocate to the town stream. We've got the vertical drop. It could work."

Harald flipped open his notebook to the page with the drawings. "It's overgrown, but what I saw looked intact."

His father smiled. "That's enough power to make a difference. We could run the workshop—bring the main lathe back online. Maybe even the bandsaw."

Harald picked up his father's enthusiasm—then paused, remembering something else. "I found something else in the workshop. There was another rifle—a shotgun. And a box of shells. I left them there, hidden."

A flicker of concern crossed Erik's face, his smile fading. "You did the right thing leaving them. There's no one on Talem who'd report it, but still... just knowing about live ammunition is dangerous. Let's keep this between us for now. We'll tell Grace—she can help us figure out what to do."

He turned, the weight in his voice easing. "Now eat up before your bread goes stale."

The gun lay on Harald's favorite bench in the workshop, parts spread out on the oil cloth he'd prepared. Mostly stripped.

The stock—a solid slab of walnut darkened with time—rested to one side, its inletting clean but dry. The air bottle, unscrewed and empty, lay next to it, still bearing the faint scuff marks of years in storage.

He'd set the breech block upright, the bolt removed and cleaned, its slim cylinder now free of grit and moving smooth under finger pressure. A pair of Allen screws sat beside the trigger unit, along with the retaining pins he'd knocked free with care. The barrel, short and thick for its caliber, was surprisingly bright inside—he'd run an oiled patch through it and found only the faintest discoloration.

On a small tray sat the fine parts: the forward valve seal, a cracked O-ring, the magazine spindle.

A nylon brush lay beside them, black with carbon. His clothes smelled faintly of oil and old grease.

He was careful not to move too quickly, not to bump the order he'd laid out—the logic of the assembly was its own kind of story.

He stood for a moment, just looking at it. The pieces alone didn't seem like much—metal and wood, simple tools shaped into something more. But the fit of it all, the way the action seated into the stock with barely a breath of tolerance, the clean line of the barrel—none of that happened by accident.

This was precision. Not showy, not ornamental. Just exact.

Harald found himself wondering about the person who last held it in working order. Someone who'd cared enough to keep it clean, maybe even to fire it with intention. Not a toy, not a leftover. A real weapon, built to last.

He exhaled slowly, looking up just as Grace wandered through the workshop door.

She walked lightly. Eyes moving over the rows of salvaged parts, half finished repairs and projects. Grace wasn't an engineer, she was a historian, but one who understood the need that was filled in the workshop. She reached Harald's bench, not surprised to see him there early in the morning. "That looks like a serious piece of history," she said, nodding to the disassembled rifle. "The curve of the stock—looks like it's from an earlier time."

"I'm hoping I can get it working, it's in good shape— better than I'd thought. It might need a new seal." Harald hesitated. "It could help with small game, supplement the traps."

"I found something else at the mansion." The gravity of the statement caused Grace to look up. "A shotgun.

And a box of live ammunition. I left it hidden but Dad says we should talk about it." Grace inclined her head and waited for him to continue. "I know that live rounds are illegal. Forbidden. But I'm not really sure why?"

She didn't answer quickly. She took a moment before her measured voice offered a history that was not a cause, but a piece of a larger collapse—one that had quietly, steadily redirected the course of the world.

"You're not wrong to ask," she said at last. "It's one thing to learn a rule. Another to understand what made it necessary."

She stepped closer, resting her hand lightly on the bench near the rifle, as if to anchor herself there.

"Things reached a tipping point. I don't know exactly when. Maybe Columbine. After that, the shootings came often—schools, concerts, grocery stores. Anywhere people gathered. Violence became... almost ordinary. And everyone wanted a gun. For protection."

Harald listened, the unfamiliar peace of the workshop holding his attention.

"But the world had already started to break. Shortages. Blackouts. A widening gap between those who had everything and those who had nothing. And those with nothing—they had guns. And they began to use them.

"The rich and powerful weren't going to stand for that. They applied pressure. The government responded.

Ammunition, not guns, was outlawed. Severe penalties. It became a capital crime."

She paused.

"It stopped some of the violence. What it couldn't stop was the slide into something else. A world of disconnection. Maybe it was inevitable."

She looked down at the disassembled rifle.

"If you want to understand more—about people, about reasons—you should spend time in the library. Start with history, then move to philosophy. Bounce between them. The answers are all there."

Harald looked at the pieces of the rifle, then at Grace. He didn't know what to say, exactly—not because he didn't understand, but because he was beginning to. Not all at once, but enough to feel some of the connections.

He nodded slowly.

"I'll go," he said. "To the library."

He wasn't sure what he was hoping to find there. But it felt like the right next step. Maybe even the necessary one.

Grace offered a parting glance, then moved on— always something more to tend to. Harald moved too. Slowly starting to reassemble the Theoben. Each part slid back into place with quiet precision, a satisfying click or turn that confirmed what he'd already suspected: the thing had been built to last. He moved with care, not rushing, letting the process guide his thoughts. The cracked O-ring replaced by a crafted rubber piece from an old inner tube.

When he finished, he wiped his hands on a rag. The gun was whole again. No longer a relic, something ready for use.

He stood and stretched, heading out into the mid-morning sunshine. The warmth felt good on his shoulders. He thought about checking on the radio room, seeing if there was anything interesting in the log. But he paused. Then strode across the road and through the door to the small island library.

The library carried the familiar scent of salt-damp wood, like every room on the island. But beneath it was another note—sunlight on old paper, as if that warmth could hold back the maritime damp.

The space was quiet and orderly. Books lined the shelves—no scattered stacks, no cluttered tables. Except one corner. There, Harald spotted his father hunched over what looked like technical diagrams, while Lina sat cross-legged on the floor, a binder labeled *Turbines* open in her lap. They spoke in low tones, focused—absorbing everything they could about hydroelectric power. When Erik looked up, his eyes widened. But it was Lina who spoke, "what are you doing here? Did you lose a bet or something?"

Harald shrugged, and stepped closer to the table glancing at the open diagrams. "Grace thought I might learn something... Reid and Marla asked if Lina and I could help with their apple harvest next week. Payment's in cider and pie."

Erik smiled without looking up. "That sounds like a fair deal."

Lina gave a mock sigh. "Guess I better find my boots."

Harald sat beside them, the morning light slanting across the pages. For now, he could sit on his questions. Maybe the library wasn't the worst place to spend some time.

CHAPTER FIVE

THEY STOOD ON A SMALL RISE overlooking what had once been the Fletcher place.

Callum leaned his bike against a fence post and walked a few steps ahead.

"This place had the best potatoes," he muttered, as much to himself as to Erik. "Melt in your mouth good. Still some apples on the orchard trees, but it's a mess now."

Erik's gaze held on the old farmhouse. What remained of the roof was thick with moss. Brambles had climbed the walls; vines twisted through broken eaves. The windows were fogged or cracked, smeared by damp and time.

"This climate reclaims quick," he said, turning to check that the kids were coming up the rise. He nodded toward the tangle that had once been pasture. "Some of those trees are Douglas fir. The farm is gone, as far as productive land goes."

Harald and Lina came up from the west road, bikes clattering over uneven gravel. Erik waited for them before continuing.

"Some of these outlying places were low priority on the early scavenging runs," he said. "We took a few things. Left more. Too far to haul much back to town."

Lina touched his sleeve. "Maybe it's still worth a look. We might find seeds, or something still growing. Tools, even—if they weren't wood-handled."

"No time this trip," Erik said. "But sure—we can schedule someone to check it out."

Callum inclined his head, already stepping back toward his bike.

"Let's get moving, then. Drop off our two farmhands at Reid and Marla's." He shot a glance at Harald and Lina. "I'm curious to see this hydro setup. Might be able to get a few more lights on in town—if it pans out."

They reached the Harrison holding by mid-morning. The trailers hitched to their bikes had added weight, slowing the ride. It would be worse going back—heavy with apples.

Reid and Marla were already waiting near the house, standing beside a jumble of gear that looked half cobbled, half ancient: tripod ladders with wide stances, a pair of battered fishing nets, and several long poles tipped with makeshift claws or baskets.

"Well, let's get to it," Reid said, not bothering with greetings. "Expected you earlier. Burning daylight."

Marla walked over to Lina and gave her a warm pat on the arm.

"Thanks for coming, dear. Reid'll show you where to start in the orchard. I'll bring out some drinks in a bit."

Callum was already unhooking the trailers from his and Erik's bikes.

"Okay if we leave these here, Reid? You and the kids can load 'em up—we'll grab them on the way back."

Erik added, "Most likely back tomorrow afternoon, if we get through everything we're planning."

He turned to Harald and Lina. "You can come back with us if you're finished—but if they need you longer, it's fine to stay the extra night. We'll see you tomorrow either way."

Reid led them into an orchard with about twenty trees, their branches heavy with mottled red and yellow fruit. Apples already carpeted the ground, the harvest a little overdue. He gave a quick rundown on the tools, how to check for bruising, how to twist the stems clean without tearing.

"I'm setting up the press," he said, nodding toward the shed at the back of the orchard. "I'll come grab the baskets as you fill them."

He disappeared down a worn path through the grass. Lina took the first tree, canvas bag slung over one shoulder, while Harald unfolded one of the three-sided ladders and headed for the higher branches.

They worked well together, moving in an easy silence that asked nothing. Around them, the orchard hummed—bees in the grass, flies circling windfall, dappled sunlight shifting through the boughs.

Lina stretched for an apple just out of reach.

"You think Reid ever smiles? Or was he born a curmudgeon?"

Harald smiled faintly. "Yeah—probably born that way."

His gaze drifted across the orchard, then up toward the farmhouse.

"Takes a certain kind of curmudgeon to keep a place like this from falling apart."

Harald thought of the old mansion. The Fletcher place. How fast it had gone—swallowed by vines, softened by rot. Keeping nature at bay was a battle, not a given. A kind of responsibility.

He was starting to understand why his father always seemed so serious.

The siblings worked easily together, no need to talk— helping each other when needed, falling into rhythm. After a while, they spotted Marla crossing the orchard toward them, tray in hand with what looked like drinks and cake.

"You two ready for a break?" she called. They both nodded, Harald stepping down from the ladder and brushing off his hands.

Now that she was closer, he could see the glasses held juice—cloudy, golden, already browning at the edges.

"Liquid gold," Marla said, handing a glass to Lina first. "Doesn't last. So drink it while it's sweet. Not too many folks get to taste apple juice anymore."

Harald took a sip. It was tart and earthy, with a trace of pulp at the bottom. Warm from the sun. He wiped his mouth with the back of his hand.

"Marla, what happens to all the apples?"

She smiled. "We press a fair bit, but juice won't keep without a fridge. Cider we can make—it ferments in the cool shed and holds through the winter. We dry some too, slice and string them, but that takes time and hands."

She nodded toward the baskets they'd half-filled. "Most of it'll go into the root cellars around town. They last... until they don't."

Lina nodded. "Like the squash harvest. Those go into the cellars too. How do you keep things from going bad?"

Marla paused, clearly considering. Lina was sharp—always had been.

"You're right, Lina. That's a whole job in itself. Making sure there's enough, but not too much. Timing it, checking for soft spots, knowing what to use first. It's not just about growing things. It's about keeping them."

They worked through into the later afternoon when the shadows began to stretch through the orchard. Marla had come and gone, pushing a creaking wheelbarrow with baskets of apples, while Reid kept at the press, working through the haul bound for cider. At last, she called up,

"That'll do for today. Come and get washed up—we'll get some dinner."

Lina reached for one last apple, "I'm beat," she said, "but that was kind of satisfying."

Harald nodded, his gaze drifting down the rows of evenly spaced trees, more than half still heavy with fruit. "Feels like we've barely made a dent."

The simple dinner—stewed root vegetables, a wedge of sharp cheese, and coarse bread—but it tasted like a feast. Marla passed around thick slices of preserved pear for dessert, and Reid said little, but served seconds.

The two children cleared the dishes and headed for the sink, Marla casting a quick glance toward Reid, her approval unspoken. No one lingered long once dinner was done. All four weary with the ache of hard work.

The sleeping loft was reached by a narrow wooden ladder tucked into the corner of the main room. As they got ready, Reid handed Harald the LED lamp he'd repaired on his last visit. Lina followed, grateful for the early bedtime.

The loft had low beams and just enough space for a few mattresses. Through the small attic window starlight filtered in. It was clean and quiet. Harald and Lina settled beneath their blankets.

"That was a good day," Lina whispered.

Harald shifted, turning to get more comfortable. "Yeah. It can be fun to work."

She was quiet for a few seconds. "What do you think about Cari?"

Harald, caught slightly off guard, answered quickly. "She knows her way around the workshop. Those fire pellets will be great this winter."

Lina sighed. "No. I mean do you like her?"

He frowned into the dark. "What? She's way older than me."

Lina snorted softly. "She just turned seventeen. You're almost sixteen. That's barely a year."

Harald didn't answer right away. The moon had risen, its light painting the rafters in soft angles. "I hadn't really thought about it like that," he said.

"Mmhmm," Lina murmured, unconvinced. She rolled onto her side, pulling the blanket up to her chin. "Well... maybe you should."

The loft grew quiet: the faint creak of a breeze and the hum of summer insects.

Harald thought of Cari—the way she stood on the dock, loose-limbed and barefoot. The way she looked at the world: curious, and a little defiant.

Maybe he should pay more attention.

CHAPTER SIX

ERIK AND CALLUM didn't show the next day as expected. The steady work of picking fruit and hauling baskets went on. By evening, their hands were sore and supper was a quiet affair. Lina worried aloud about her father, but both Harald and Reid reassured her—Erik knew what he was doing, and with Callum along, they were certain to see them the following day.

The next morning, just as breakfast was being served, the two men wandered into the kitchen. They were filthy and bone-tired, but both wore faint smiles as Marla greeted them and ushered them to seats at the farm table.

Harald was full of questions, but Marla quieted him with a gentle, "Let them eat first."

They ate ravenously after two nights of rough camping and meager rations. When the plates were nearly clean, Callum leaned forward, eager to share.

"We found the turbine and generator. Both intact. The wiring's brittle, but the whole thing is salvageable."

Lina leaned in. "What took so long? We were worried when you didn't come back yesterday."

Erik's eyes softened. "Sorry, Lina—I knew you'd be worried. We needed more time to get everything moved out of the stream. It's all down near the beach now."

Callum picked up the thread. "Everything's staged and ready. We're going to have to bring the old barge up from town—no way we're hauling it ten miles by hand. It's at Wren Beach. More of a cove than a beach really—nice and sheltered. Great place to land the barge."

Erik nodded. "It'll take coordination. We'll need bodies, and we'll have to wait for the tides to cooperate."

Then he looked up, a grin spreading across his face. "This is going to make a difference—for everyone on Talem."

Reid stretched the word with mock exasperation. "Well... if you're not too tired, we could use a hand finishing the last of the apples."

With the extra help, the work went quickly. By midday, four bikes stood ready, each with a trailer full of apples for the trek back to town.

As Harald and Lina wheeled their bikes toward the road, Erik turned to Marla.

"We should talk before we head out."

She nodded, already sensing where this was going.

"Marla, how would you feel about spending the winter in town this year?" Erik kept his tone even. "Not much farm work to do in the cold months. We can make you comfortable—and you'd be around people."

Before Marla could answer, Reid muttered, "Not much use to anyone sitting around down there."

Erik didn't look away. "Reid, there's plenty that needs doing in town. Especially in winter. We can always use more hands."

"I've got another suggestion that might help," Erik said. He was pressing now, but went on. "Peter could come up next month for a few days. Help out. Might make things go a little easier."

Reid didn't answer right away. He looked at the full baskets, the three-legged ladders waiting to be hauled back to the barn.

"He's young," he said at last.

"He's willing," Marla added quietly.

Reid gave a grunt—somewhere between agreement and resignation. "We'll talk about it."

The road back climbed gently through the lower woods, then leveled out as it broke from the coast and turned inland. The trailers rolled behind them—heavy with apples, their frames creaking and bouncing under the strain. What had been slow going on the way out felt even slower now. Harald's legs were heavy, dulled by work and the weight of the full baskets.

He pedaled up alongside his father. Neither spoke. The rhythm of the ride settled between them. As the trees thinned and a patch of blue sky opened above, Harald broke the silence.

"How long till we can get it running?"

Erik waited a few pedal strokes before answering. "Depends on a few things. The hardest part is moving it. The install'll take time too. Could be a few weeks—if we're lucky."

"Harald," Erik said, his tone cautious now, "I've been thinking. Maybe we build a second. Replicate the design—two systems running in parallel."

Harald glanced over. "Another turbine?"

"Yeah. We'd have to fabricate, but if we can power the workshop, we can run the heavy tools."

Harald took it in. He could see it already: the turbine anchored in the stream, cables tucked beneath stone, current humming through wire. A rhythm pacing quicker, feeding more life into the island. More possibility for Talem.

The road dropped back into town, a return to civilization after the quiet of the orchard and farm. Voices carried on the air—snatches of conversation, the rhythm of daily life. A few children played tag near the library. A couple chatted as they hauled supplies from the warehouse by the docks.

Harald took it in—the familiar clutter, the movement, the voices. Home.

Grace sat outside the meeting hall as they passed, a thin paperback folded in her lap.

"Back in one piece," she called, closing the book. Her eyes moved from Erik to Harald, then settled on the trailer. "That looks promising."

"We excavated the turbine," Erik said. "Generator's intact. We moved it down near the beach—everything's staged and ready."

Grace nodded but didn't smile. "And now?"

"Now we bring it back to life," Erik said. "Maybe more than that. If it works, we're thinking of building a second."

She stepped closer, her voice low so only Erik could hear. "Just be careful, Erik. Growth isn't always progress. You know what happens when systems get ahead of reasons."

Erik reached out, resting a hand lightly on her arm. "I do, Grace. We'll think it through. No missteps."

Harald didn't hear the words, but he caught the tone—the way Grace leaned in, the measure in Erik's reply. It wasn't about the machines. That was the point.

He looked toward the harbor. Waves pushed gently against the dock wall. The dock didn't move.

CHAPTER SEVEN

HARALD ARRIVED AT THE BREAKFAST TABLE later than usual. The orchard work still clung to his limbs—stiff and slow. At the range, Lina was turning a giant porcini, its cap nearly the size of a saucer. The smell drew him closer. She crumbled goat cheese into the mushroom's sizzling center, the edges just beginning to crisp.

"Morning lazy bones," she chided. "This one's mine. You can go next."

Harald sat heavily, "I think I'll start with some tea." His voice matched his limbs—barely working.

Erik was already at the table, tide charts spread before him, pencil tapping in thought. "Looks like there's a good window in a couple of days to get the barge up the coast," he said. "I'll need both of you on this one."

After breakfast, Lina stood and packed a few snacks— toasted nuts, slivers of dried apple, some flatbread and cheese wrapped in cloth.

"These dried apples are good, Harald—if you and apples are still talking." She moved toward the door.

"Mushroom pan's on you today. I'm headed to the greenhouse."

Harald watched his sister go. Some days were easier than others with that one.

He turned to his father, who was still absorbed in his notebook and often seemed oblivious to his children's exchanges.

"I'm at the workshop first," Harald said. "Then I'll do the well checks from Highpoint. Do you need anything today?"

Erik, eyes still on the tide charts, nodded faintly. "No, Harald. I'll see you later. Have a good day."

The workshop door creaked as Harald stepped inside. He made a note to oil the hinges before leaving, then moved toward his bench. The Theoben caught his eye—resting where he'd left it, matte stock and long barrel, unmistakable.

He wasn't alone. Cari was already at her station, bent over a hinge assembly, sleeves rolled, hands smudged with graphite.

She looked up as he entered.

He felt his face warm—embarrassed, though he couldn't say why.

"You alright, Harald? What's up—did you run here?"

"No," he said. "Just... morning."

Harald crossed to his bench, where the wheelbarrow frame still sat. A few others drifted in during the morning. You didn't need to book time—there was always room.

When he'd tightened the last bolt. The wheel turned smoothly as he gave it a test push. Something useful, something finished.

He turned to Cari. "You want to shoot for a bit?"

She looked over, curious. "The Theoben?"

"Yeah. I made a few test pellets before I went to Reid and Marla's, but didn't have time to try them out." He smiled. "First time I've fired it. Might be a little risky."

Cari laughed, and Harald grabbed the rifle as they headed for the door.

"You know," he said, "we could probably use a real range. Permanent."

They followed the path down to the usual shooting spot, the trees thinning as the clearing opened ahead. Harald propped a slab of driftwood against a stump and stepped back. He checked the rifle, running a hand along the cool barrel, checking the sight, then offered it to Cari.

"Why don't you take the first shot?"

"You afraid it might explode?" she said, raising an eyebrow—but she took the rifle and walked thirty paces back from the target.

Cari lifted the rifle to her shoulder and took a slow breath. The first shot cracked—louder than expected—the pellet missing just wide of the target.

She lowered the rifle, blinking. "Okay. That's... not what I expected."

Harald grinned. "Bit of a kick for air power."

Cari studied the gun, adjusted the rear sight, then raised it again. This time, the pellet struck dead center. The slab of driftwood split with a dry crack.

They both stared.

"Here, pass it over," Harald said, reaching for the rifle. "I need a go at that."

Harald took his turn, the stock snug against his shoulder. Two shots—both just wide of the target, but close enough.

He exhaled and turned to Cari. "I'm headed up to Highpoint. Would you mind taking it back to the shop?"

She nodded and took the Theoben from him.

Harald hesitated, then added, "We should probably think about making more pellets—and setting that thing under lock and key."

Cari gave a thoughtful nod. "Yeah. That's a great idea. That gun's a tool."

Harald swung by the radio room, offered Sarah a quick greeting, and grabbed the handheld and the log for well checks. He moved fast toward the summit, head down. Fog lay thick across the channel—no view to the mainland today.

For some reason, he felt like hurrying through the check—his mind elsewhere.

But Reid and Marla had other ideas.

Marla must've been waiting for the call. She asked about the ride back, about the apples—were they in storage yet?

And his sister.

He took a breath.

Okay. Slow down.

The last call came from the Conways, all the way out on east road. It was Kiernan checking in.

"Pretty good here, Highpoint. One thing—we've all had some... tummy issues recently. Had the same thing for twenty-four hours last week too."

The radio went quiet for a moment.

"Maybe you should tell the docs. Just give them a heads-up."

Harald made a note in the log. His father wanted a record—always.

Kiernan switched topics, breaking radio protocol.

"Harald, can you remind your dad about the fertilizer? We need it. Like yesterday."

Harald added a note about the fertilizer to the log. He'd tell the docs about the sickness .

Probably nothing to worry about.

But if Kiernan thought they should know...

Easy enough to swing by the clinic on the way back to the radio room.

The clinic was quiet when Harald stepped in. The air smelled faintly of antiseptic, but the overlay was herbal.

Hamish glanced up from the desk, scribbling notes on old ledger paper. He smiled at Harald—his irrepressible good nature the thing Harald liked most about him.

He'd been a med student once, a few months shy of a qualification that no longer mattered.

"Coming off checks?" he asked, eyeing the radio in Harald's hand.

"Yeah. The last one was Kiernan Conway. Says they've had some stomach trouble. Nothing serious, but it's happened a couple of times."

Hamish scratched at his stubble. "Could've been something they ate, but could be water. I'll mention it to Jana."

Harald nodded. Jana, Hamish's partner, balanced his easygoing nature with an intellect shaped in her past life. A researcher—biochem or something—Jana liked to look for answers.

"She's been saying something's off along the east coast," Hamish added. "Algae, or bloom runoff maybe. We'll take a look."

Hamish turned back to his notes, already half-absorbed.

Sarah smiled as Harald stepped into the radio room. "Perfect timing," she said, rising from the chair. "I need to duck out early. Callum should be here in about a half hour. Think you can cover the shortwave till then?"

Harald nodded. "Sure."

She gave him a grateful pat on the arm as she passed. "Appreciate it."

Harald settled into the chair. He liked the feel of the radio room—the low hum of equipment and the faint hiss of open channels. It felt alive in its own way. A place of listening. Of possibility. News from outside, maybe.

He opened the logbook. Several contacts today. One entry caught his eye: *Drifter.*

No reply had been logged.

He adjusted the dials and tuned to the frequency of the last contact.

At first, just static. Then faintly, he heard it.

"...repeat, this is Drifter. Anyone copy?"

Harald leaned forward and keyed the mic. "Station receiving," he said. "Go ahead, Drifter."

A pause, then a voice—steady but strained.

"Didn't expect anyone. Thanks for answering."

"No problem," Harald replied. "What's your status, Drifter?"

"We're moored inland. On a barge. Parents left yesterday morning to look for food. Still not back."

The headset hissed as Drifter cut his mic, then came back on. "We're stuck here. No fuel. No way back to the coast."

Harald kept his voice calm. "You're not alone, Drifter."

"My name's Mark. I've got two sisters here, but I'm worried about my folks. It's not safe out there. The army's everywhere, food is rationed. People are desperate."

Harald let out a slow breath. "Copy that, Mark. I hear you. That's a lot to bear."

"Just needed to say it out loud, I guess," Mark said. "Didn't think anyone was out there."

Harald rubbed his temple. "I'm listening," he said. "You're not completely alone. We're monitoring channels all day. My name's Harald."

Mark was quiet, but when he spoke again, his voice had softened. "Thanks. Thanks, Harald."

The static faded. Harald sat for a moment, staring at the logbook without seeing it.

The door creaked open. Callum stepped in, unbuttoning his jacket. "Hey, sorry I'm late."

Harald pulled off the headset. "No problem."

Callum glanced at him, then at the log. "You okay?"

Harald hesitated, then gave a nod. "Got a call from a kid on a barge. Parents went to find food. Haven't come back."

Callum sighed. "Damn. Let's note it in the log. We'll try to follow up."

He caught Harald's eye. "It's tough out there. This is why we man the comms."

Harald stepped out into the late afternoon light. He headed to the beach, soft needles underfoot on the worn path. More often than not, town folk gathered as the sun set—a time to be together, to share what little there was.

Tonight, he wanted that. The company. The comfort of it.

When he reached the shore, a small fire was already burning—driftwood and pinecones. Harald sat a little apart, but close enough to feel the connection.

A few minutes passed before Grace eased down beside him, drawing up her knees and placing a hand lightly on his arm.

Harald sat in the silence. Then, tentatively, he spoke. "There must be lots of people out there. Alone." He turned to face her. "I spoke with a boy on the radio. His parents are missing."

Grace met his gaze and gently squeezed his arm. "Maybe I'll tell a story."

Harald inclined his head. "One of your old ones?"

She gave a faint smile. "An ancient one."

Grace spoke: "Once, there were twelve villages."

The firelight crackled. Around them, the beach had quieted. A few heads turned.

"Each of the twelve villages had its own fire, and each fire was different. Some were built on driftwood and seaweed, others on coal and stone. One burned blue, and another burned tall and golden. A few were small and steady—fed by sticks, tended with care.

"At first, the fires were used for warmth and light and food. But over time, they became more. The villagers began to believe their fires were signals. A way to say: *We're still here.* As long as the fires burned, they felt safe.

"Sometimes a fire would burn brighter. Sometimes some would smolder.

"But when a fire went out, that was a time to notice. The other villages noticed. They sent help. They sent their strongest. They relit the fire.

"It became a kind of pact—unwritten but known. Your fire mattered, and so did your neighbor's. Everyone watched the hills at night for signs. Everyone kept a little extra dry wood, just in case.

"And so, even through storms and long winters, the twelve fires stayed lit.

"Not always bright. Not always strong.

"But always watched, and never alone."

CHAPTER EIGHT

THE WIND HAD STARTED just before first light, rising from a murmur to a steady push through the trees. Erik stood at the table, scanning tide charts, his plan to retrieve the hydro put on hold.

"We'll need to wait on that," he said, tapping the map. "Tides'll still work in a couple days."

He pivoted quickly. "Why don't you two go pick up the fertilizer from Kingsley today?"

Harald and Lina exchanged a look.

"Take the lugger," Erik went on. "It's blowing hard, but it'll be a quick run out and back."

Harald and Lina headed to the workshop to collect drybags and shovels. Kingsley—known to most now as Fertilizer Island—was uninhabited, but thick with seabirds. Their guano made for rich, potent fertilizer, ideal for nourishing the island's crops.

Cari was already at her bench when they arrived, sleeves rolled, hands busy with some half-finished project. Harald went straight for the drybags, but Lina veered toward her. Within moments, the two were deep in conversation, voices low, laughter flickering between them.

Harald heard the murmurs, then laughter—both girls' voices rising with excitement, then dropping again.

Lina walked over. "Change of plan. I need to help Sarah re-pot some herbs. Cari doesn't mind going for the fertilizer." Her gaze flicked to Cari, just for a moment. "Don't worry, I'll let Dad know."

Harald grunted. He wasn't sure what had just happened—but he knew he wasn't part of it. Still, Cari was a good sailor. They'd make short work of the run. Probably be back at the workshop after lunch.

They headed for the dock, Harald carrying two bags and a shovel. The Drascombe Lugger waited, tied to the pier—safe and steady, its two masts rocking gently with the tide. With the breeze gusting to twenty knots, it might even be fun.

But Cari had other ideas.

She tugged Harald toward the launch ramp. "Let's take the Lasers. This wind is perfect. We'll be there in half the time."

She flashed him a grin. "I'll race you there... and back."

Harald shrugged. Island kids grew up on the water. He'd been sailing since he could walk. Cari just happened to be faster, louder—and usually right.

He followed her to the ramp.

The dinghies were quick to rig—single sail, nothing fancy. Harald slid the rudder into the stern catches and gave it a firm push. He'd already lashed the guano sacks and shovel tight to the mast. The extra prep gave Cari a small head start.

The breeze held steady—twenty knots, maybe more. A single tack would carry them almost straight to Kingsley, the mainsail taut and full, wind on the beam.

Cari was right. Perfect conditions for the Laser.

Now she ran ahead. He knew the race had started back at the dock.

Harald settled in. Tightened the sheet—just enough. No luff. He pulled the centerboard clear of the water.

Then it came: that sound. The thrum as the boat rose to a plane, skipping across the waves, speed lifting it just enough to feel like flight.

Harald grinned. In moments like this, nothing else existed. Nothing else compared.

He'd almost caught her once—but the outcome had been decided back on Talem.

Sand and gravel crunched under his hull as he beached the Laser. Cari had already hauled hers above the high tide line, sail loose, gear stowed.

"Almost had you," Harald called, half-heartedly. "I think the shovel and bags slowed me down."

Cari smirked and helped pull his boat up beside hers. "Haven't been here in ages," she said. "Let's check it out."

The island was small compared to Talem—just a rocky outcrop three miles west, thick with seabirds.

Today, as they wandered the shoreline, it was also thick with seals.

"I don't remember this many," Cari said, eyes scanning the crowded rocks. "What do you think, Harald?"

She was right. The last time he'd been out here, there'd only been a handful.

"I think," he said slowly, "the world's adjusting. Fewer people, more seals. Maybe that's the new balance."

Cari stepped closer to the water, watching a pair of seals slip sleekly into the shallows. She nodded, almost to herself.

"It feels natural," she said. "This wild place full of wild creatures. Like it's always meant to be this way."

She glanced back at him. "Maybe we're the strange ones now."

They got to work collecting the fertilizer bound for the Conway farm. Harald shoveled while Cari held the bags open, steady against the wind.

The guano was everywhere—thick white drifts crusted over the rocks, easy to gather but pungent.

Harald clipped the last bag shut, twisting the top and cinching it tight.

Cari was staring west.

He followed her gaze—storm clouds stacking along the horizon, dark and heavy, threat becoming reality.

"We'd better head back," he said, trying to play down his concern.

By the time they reached the boats, the first drops were falling. Rain turned to a sheet, and the wind began to howl.

It was Cari who said it first. "We need to wait this one out."

Harald was already hauling the boats higher, pulling them clear of the surging tide.

"Maybe it'll just blow through," he said, raising his voice over the wind. "We can shelter—I know a sea cave on the far side of the cove. Should keep us dry, and out of the worst of it."

The cave wasn't deep, but the rock overhang kept most of the rain off. Water dripped steadily from the lip above, pooling in the dark patches of sand near their feet.

They huddled just inside, sitting on dry rocks, wet hair clinging to their faces. Cari's cheeks flushed from the wind.

"Well," she said, pulling her knees up. "So much for a quick trip."

Harald managed a crooked smile. "We've had worse ideas."

For a while, they just listened—the rush of rain on rock, the occasional boom of distant surf. The storm was close now, but not angry. Just big.

Cari leaned back, resting on her hands. "Feels like the island's holding its breath."

Harald didn't know what to say to that. He nodded, eyes on the mouth of the cave, where the sea churned gray and white.

She looked at him then—not teasing, not performing. Just looked.

"You're more thoughtful than I expected," she said.

He met her eyes. "You're a faster sailor than I expected."

That got a smile. But it didn't fade.

She shifted, and before he could think too much about it, she was leaning in, slow and certain.

When their lips touched, it was soft. Not dramatic. Not even planned. Just a moment—warm, human, and real—cutting through the storm outside.

They didn't say anything right away. Sat, side by side, listening to the storm ease around them.

Cari leaned back against the rock wall, her knees still pulled close, eyes half-closed. Harald watched the mouth of the cave, where the sea was beginning to settle, the horizon softening under a break in the clouds.

After a while, she spoke, voice quiet. "If the break holds, we might catch a breeze home."

Harald nodded. "Yeah."

But neither of them moved.

The wind was back—gentler now, steady but kind.

They rigged the Lasers in silence, pushed off together, and let the sails fill. The boats gently keeping pace as Talem came closer.

By the time they reached the dock, the sun was heading low. Lina was waiting. Balanced on a piling, skipping stones into the harbor.

She looked up as they pulled in. One glance at their faces, and her mouth curled into the smallest smile.

"Took your time," she said.

CHAPTER NINE

THE RIVER WAS A WIDE BROWN RIBBON. Barely moving. The banks overcrowded with willow and alder. The barge rocked gently at the mooring, tethered to a broken tree, angled out crossways from the embankment.

Mark crouched on the deck, watching, waiting.

He made a list in his head. What did they have left? A couple of dented cans, some rice cakes, a few sprouting potatoes. Not enough.

Inside the cabin Loretta was reading. A book she'd read before, and hopefully would again. Lisa had fallen asleep up against her. Wrapped in a blanket. Her thumb still inside her mouth. Their cheeks were thin, not sunken. Still color in them, still time.

His mother's words hung heavy: *Don't move the barge. It's hidden. We'll be back, tomorrow at the latest.*

That had been three days ago.

They'd left early, just past sunrise, when the mist was drifting. Their packs were empty in hopes of stuffing them with something, anything edible. Maybe government rations. Perhaps an abandoned garden, where rows were left untended. It didn't matter. There was no food left on the barge, they had to do something.

Mark rose and stepped into the cabin.

Loretta looked up. "They're still not back?"

Mark shook his head.

Lisa stirred then settled.

"They said not to move."

"I know."

"But—what if something happened?"

Mark didn't answer.

Outside a river rat slipped into the water with a swash.

He stared out of the cabin window, to the bank, beyond to the trees.

"I think..." he started then stopped. His voice felt harsh in the stillness.

Loretta waited.

"I think, if they're not back by morning. We need to go."

She nodded. Not in agreement. More like she understood. He'd already decided.

CHAPTER TEN

THE WATER WAS CLEAR AND COLD, a gentle lapping that shifted the tendrils of eelgrass. Lina stood in the shallows, Jana nearby—a vial in one hand, a small net in the other. They had waded in knee-deep, far enough that the chill settled into their legs and the shoreline runoff was behind them. Jana wanted samples from multiple depths, from water that still moved.

"I used to do a lot of this with grad students," Jana said, swirling a sample slowly.

Lina carried the field pack reversed across her chest, vials clinking softly inside. She liked being here, helping. Jana's focus made her feel steadier somehow.

"This beats hauling dirty old hydro gear from the shore to a boat," Lina said. She'd been relieved when Jana asked her to join—and Cari had been more than happy to trade places, heading out with Harald and the others to retrieve the unit.

Jana nodded. "If they get it working, it could really change things. More light. Maybe refrigeration again. It'd help us at the clinic."

"What do you think you're going to find in the samples?" Lina asked.

Jana turned, handing over a full vial. "We'll take a look under the microscope when we get back. Why don't you plan on sticking around? I can show you how we do it."

Lina marked the sample, writing as Jana instructed: Eelgrass zone, Level: surface.

She liked being useful—following her curiosity to understand how and why things were done. Jana seemed to respond to that. Maybe that's why she'd asked Lina along.

Lina screwed the cap on tight and tucked the vial into the padded slot. She was reaching for a fresh one when Jana paused.

"Hang on," Jana said, staring at a stretch of water just past the eelgrass. "That doesn't look right."

Lina followed her gaze. A faint film rode the surface. She wouldn't have noticed it on her own—but Jana was right. Something oily. Greasy. Floating in slow spirals.

"That's not just algae," Jana murmured. "See how it clings?"

Lina leaned closer. It wasn't green, exactly—more of a dull tan. Something that didn't belong in the water.

"What is it?" she asked.

"Could be from one of the farms upstream. Maybe livestock waste, if they haven't been careful with the composting protocols."

She scraped a sample into a new vial. "Label that one: *Surface anomaly, east shore.*"

They headed back to the shore, samples packed away. Jana scanned the slope above the beach. The view was green and orderly—a pair of goats grazing gently in the long grass, late-season crops set in a tidy field. Her eyes followed a footpath winding between two homesteads, both well kept and sheltered from the weather that moved in relentlessly from the west.

The other coast was wild. The road there had long since turned to trail—reclaimed by root and rain. But Jana knew: appearances could deceive. The farms here could be just as hard on the land. And the sea.

She would run the samples. Check if it was a bloom, or a compost leak. Follow the clues.

The hydro team was back at the dock by midday. The retrieval had gone smoothly—the steady onshore breeze pushing the lugger along the shoreline, with Cari and Harald sailing ahead in the small craft, towing the barge behind them, its deck crowded with salvaged pipe, fittings, and the turbine generator from the old plant.

They finished unloading the last of the equipment from the barge, and Erik handed Harald a notepad.

"Take this to Supply," he said. "We'll need it this afternoon if we want the install moving tomorrow."

Harald glanced at the page—his father's familiar, blocky script. The letters were clean and purposeful. The list included cable brackets, mounting clamps, sealing compound, and a bunch of other things he didn't even recognize.

"Tommy'll be down there," Erik added. "He'll find it all."

Harald nodded and set off toward the row of old, weather-streaked warehouses. Once, these buildings had buzzed with activity—processing the fish hauled in from trawlers. That was long ago.

It was Grace who had brought order to the ruins. She and a few others had cleared out the space, installed shelving, and devised a way to track every piece of salvage added to inventory. She used what she knew: the Dewey Decimal system. Repurposed from old-world libraries, adapted to a new kind of knowledge. Every item coded—by name, by use, by potential.

Supply was a vault. Not just a place for spare parts, but the bones of a different kind of future. The materials here could sustain life on Talem for decades—maybe longer.

Inside, the air was cooler—wooden rafters above, shelves rising in long, orderly rows. Sunlight filtered through the high windows, catching dust motes that drifted among the beams like tiny feathers floating skyward.

The scent of the warehouse was tinged with machine oil and salt. A faint trace of long-departed fish still lingered.

"Looking for something?"

A voice from the rows.

Tommy emerged, wiping his hands on his apron. A headlamp perched on his brow. His unkempt beard was streaked with wire filings.

"Erik sent me," Harald said, holding out the notepad.

Tommy took it, scanned the page once—then again, slower the second time.

"Hydro install," he said.

Harald nodded.

Without another word, Tommy turned and moved down the aisle with quiet efficiency, pulling items and dropping them into a wooden cart he kept at his side.

"You know where everything is?" Harald asked, a little in awe.

"I try," Tommy said. "Could always use an extra pair of hands, Harald—if you've got spare time."

As they turned the corner, Harald spotted something he didn't recognize on a low shelf. Bright orange plastic, rounded on one end, with a small crank handle on top.

He picked it up. "What's this?"

Tommy glanced back. "Pasta machine."

Harald frowned. "Pasta?"

"Yeah. Manual roller. Found it in a holiday rental up the coast."

Harald turned the crank once. It squeaked, uselessly.

Tommy shrugged. "Seems pointless, I know. But we keep it all. You never know when someone'll come needing exactly that. If we've still got it, it's here—logged and entered into inventory."

He turned back toward the shelves. "That's the deal."

When Harald got back to the dock with the cart, a small crowd had gathered. Erik stood off to one side, arms crossed. Callum was nearby, one hand lifted in a vague gesture of calm toward a few agitated townsfolk.

"...Top priority for more power needs to be hot water—"

"—if we can get some refrigeration, it helps everyone. Produce will last longer—"

Harald slowed his steps, listening.

"What about the clinic?" someone called out. "Hamish could use the dental drill. That's a game changer."

That quieted things for a moment. Then Callum spoke, voice low but firm: "It won't run everything. This power is incremental." He caught Erik's gaze. "It can help move us along, but it's not a magic wand."

Before anyone could reply, another voice cut through—calm and steady, clear and confident.

"Let's not fight over something we haven't built yet."

Heads turned. Grace stood at the edge of the crowd, her gaze moving slowly from face to face. She wore her wide-brimmed hat—the one she always reached for when she wasn't sure how long she'd be outdoors.

"Power is a tool," she said, her voice deliberate. "But tools can change us. We've spoken of this before."

Her eyes found Erik. He met the look with a slight lift of his chin—acknowledgment, nothing more.

"Let's get it installed. Let's see what it can give us. Then we'll meet. In the library. We'll weigh what matters most—what helps the many, what sustains."

She paused.

"We've managed without shortcuts. A little patience will serve us now."

The silence that followed wasn't exactly agreement, but the mood had shifted. Softer. More contained.

Harald exhaled, only then realizing he'd been holding his breath.

Jana and Lina walked the east road back to town, headed for the clinic.

"First thing," Jana said, "let's look at the anomaly sample. Hamish might have some ideas too."

Hamish was finishing up with a twelve-year-old who'd skinned his knee, tying off a piece of fresh gauze. He peeled off a glove and gave them a nod as they entered.

"How was the east shore?"

Jana unslung the sample bag from her shoulder. "We collected everything we needed. But saw something that's... concerning."

She set the vial on the counter. The tan slick still clung to the inside surface, faint but persistent.

Hamish leaned in, gave it a cautious sniff, and raised an eyebrow. "That's not runoff."

"It doesn't match any of the compost indicators I've seen," Jana said. "But we'll know more in a moment."

She moved to the microscope near the back table, clicked on the solar lamp, and began prepping a slide. Lina stood nearby, arms folded across her chest.

When both clinicians had viewed the sample, Jana waved Lina over.

"See the fast-moving, rod-shaped bacteria? Likely E. coli. This isn't compost—it's got bacterial overgrowth, particulate fat... see that sheen?"

She glanced at Hamish. "We need to stop anyone harvesting shellfish along the east shore."

Hamish placed a hand on the table, his fingers tightening slightly. "We're going to have to look at all those farms. Someone's leaking sewage—hopefully accidental. If it isn't..."

He let the thought hang for a moment.

"...we've got a bigger problem."

Hamish stepped away from the table, already reaching for a notepad.

"I'll write up a summary," he said. "If this is coming from one of the farms, we'll need a plan. Coordinated visits. We might have to shut off water. I'll put it in plain language."

"Would you run it to Erik, let Grace know?"

Lina nodded. "Sure."

Hamish gave her a small smile. "It'll carry more weight coming from someone who saw the sample in the water."

By late afternoon the following day, the work was about finished.

The pipe had been laid, the generator mounted in the new housing Erik and Callum had rigged from salvaged framing. Harald checked the electrical connections with a handheld meter, the wires running from the intake channel down to the distribution box.

The crew was focused—just the occasional instruction or whispered question. It was the kind of work that pulled people together: shared, physical, purposeful. A clear objective, reached through collaboration and grit.

When the final cable was locked into place, Erik gave a short nod.

Harald closed the breaker.

At first, only the sound of water rushing through the channel. Then a low hum—soft and mechanical—rose from the generator housing. The hum grew into a purring spin, pulsed once, then steadied. It wasn't loud, but it added a new frequency to the air, tuned into motion.

No cheers. But the glances passed among the team spoke of satisfaction—and now, possibility.

They were still gathered near the channel when Peter appeared at the edge of the slope. He lifted a hand in greeting as he approached, walking quickly toward the group.

Erik turned first. "Something?"

Peter nodded, his eyes landing on Harald. "Drifter called in. Just a brief one."

That got everyone's attention.

Sarah had followed Peter down. She stepped forward, her expression unreadable. "He's moving the barge."

"Where?" Harald asked, his voice rising slightly.

Peter shook his head. "Didn't say. But there's only one way it's going to move—downstream. He said he'd call again when they were settled."

Silence followed.

Only the sound of the channel now—the rush of water, and the steady whirr of the generator filling the space between them.

CHAPTER ELEVEN

HARALD AND CARI sat beneath the library's tall south window, knees touching, poring over a heavy book Harald balanced on his leg. Morning light streamed in, spilling across the pages.

"Pasta," Harald said, tracing a finger beneath the word. "It's basically flour and water. That's it. Maybe an egg if you want to get fancy."

Cari leaned closer. The old cookbook was coming apart at the spine. Creased corners and smudge marks freckled the yellowing pages—photographs of tagliatelle and linguine smothered in cream and tomato sauces.

"You knead it, rest it, roll it out. Cut it into shapes and boil. That's it." Harald's voice carried his excitement. "We even have one of these in Supply," he said, pointing to a diagram of a hand-crank roller.

She looked at him. "You're telling me we could actually make this?"

"We *are* going to make this," he said. "I'm serious."

Cari grinned, her hand brushing Harald's knee. "I'm getting hungry just reading about it."

Harald gently closed the cookbook, careful not to stress the spine. "They worked out some kind of power-sharing agreement last night. Good news for the workshop—it'll get power guaranteed in the mornings."

"That's great," Cari said. "What about the clinic? And hot showers?"

"Not sure about the hot showers," Harald replied, narrowing his eyes, unsure if she was serious. "They're calling it flexible rotation. One line powered at a time. Batteries get topped up at night. The clinic definitely gets a window."

"Guaranteed charging," Cari echoed. "That feels like a game changer for anything that needs constant power."

"You're right. Jana is working on refrigeration—for the clinic, but also something the community can use for food. Stretch the harvest window a little. A step up from the root cellars."

Cari nodded. "Maybe this could help with comms too. So we don't have to hike to Highpoint every time there's a message."

Before Harald could answer, the library door creaked open. Lina stepped in, books clutched under one arm, fighting a grin at the sight of them.

"There you are," she said, eyeing them with mock suspicion. "What have you done to my brother? He's turning into a bookworm."

Harald rolled his eyes as Lina dropped her books onto a nearby table. Cari just smiled.

"Anyway," Lina continued, "there's news from Highpoint. Peter picked up a message—Nameth's sending a boat this afternoon."

She gave them a pointed look. "You two might want to relocate your little love fest down to the dock."

Harald exchanged a quick look with Cari, then stood to return the cookbook. Nameth rarely visited—and never without a reason.

"Guess we're done with pasta for now," he said quietly.

A small crowd had already gathered at the dock by the time they arrived—half the town, it seemed. Children perched on crates, craning for a better view. The older residents stood with arms folded, their expressions somewhere between wary and curious.

Harald peered past the harbor wall. The sea was calm, a slate mirror stretched to the horizon. The sound came first—unmistakable. A low thud, rising steadily: a combustion engine.

Heads turned. Murmurs rippled through the crowd. Harald caught Erik and Grace exchanging a glance.

A white motorboat crested the inlet, speed steady and measured—as if to say, *here I am.*

The boat entered the harbor, throttle easing back, its wake folding inward behind it. Harald counted four figures.

At the helm stood Frank Wells, his windbreaker zipped to the neck, one hand steady on the throttle.

In the stern sat two strangers. One was short and stocky, eyes scanning the dock like a soldier surveying terrain. Beside him, a tall, gaunt woman watched the crowd with a fixed, unreadable stare.

Standing just behind Frank was a girl about Harald's age. Bree.

The boat idled forward and touched the dock with a soft nudge. No one moved to catch a line—and Frank didn't seem to expect it.

It took a moment, but then Callum stepped forward.

"Hello Frank, to what do we owe the honor?"

"Callum. Good to see you."

Frank looked past him to the gathered crowd, nodding slightly. "Didn't mean to cause a stir. Things on Nameth are going well. We just wanted to make some time to talk in person."

He paused—just a beat too long.

"That said, we've had a few odd stomach cases on the island. Probably nothing, but we wondered if Jana or Hamish might have some ideas."

"And while we're here, we've been working on recommissioning the old phone lines. Most of the infrastructure's still intact. It'd be good to talk more directly. We'd need your help with that."

The words hung in the air. Then Frank stepped back from the helm and nodded for the others to climb up to the dock.

Harald watched and wondered. A phone connection between the islands—that was interesting.

But the stomach issues? That suggested something else. Something that tied the islands together in a different way.

Callum led the group up toward the meeting hall. "Let's talk more inside."

As they moved away from the dock, Bree fell in beside Harald.

"How are things going, Mr. Highpoint Well Check?"

He'd suspected as much. Unicorn Six, loud and proud.

Of course it was Bree—Frank Wells' daughter. She looked the same mostly. That streak in her hair though, that was new.

As they neared the steps of the meeting hall, Frank fell in beside Callum.

"Would you mind if we spoke privately for a few minutes before the full meeting?"

Callum didn't break stride. "We don't really do private, Frank. Not when it concerns the whole island."

Frank gave a short nod, but his eyes flicked sideways—calculating. "Of course. Just thought it might be easier to speak leader to leader."

Callum let out a breath, somewhere between a laugh and a sigh. "That's another thing—we don't do titles much either."

Harald, trailing a few steps behind, had heard the exchange. Callum's response was matter-of-fact. Things didn't operate behind closed doors on Talem.

Frank's face hadn't changed, but something in his posture had tightened.

The islanders pulled their chairs into a loose semicircle, facing three set aside for the Nameth guests. Bree had somehow slipped among the local crowd and looked to be making her way toward Harald.

It was Frank who spoke first as the room settled.

"I'd like to introduce you to Clare Drew. Clare came to Nameth from the mainland about a year ago. We've been working on some things over there. Clare can tell you more."

Clare stood. Her body was tall and angular, her expression composed but alert.

"Thank you, Mayor Wells."

Harald noticed she didn't even glance in the mayor's direction.

"I've been working closely with the leadership on Nameth since I arrived—on ideas particularly suited to communities like these."

Out of the corner of his eye, Harald saw Grace shift in her seat.

Clare let the silence stretch just long enough to feel intentional.

"We're moving toward a cooperative structure on the island. Something more efficient. Something that benefits all inhabitants."

She scanned the room, eyes steady.

"We've made the decision to abandon our outlying farms—for now—and concentrate all our people and efforts in one place."

"With one large farm operating efficiently, we can easily feed our entire population. We'll have excess—and we're more than willing to... trade."

She let that word settle before going on.

"All our people are behind this. We live communally, together. This is the best direction for our immediate future."

Harald studied Clare as she spoke. Her tone was calm, confident—too confident, maybe. The kind of certainty that left little room for questions.

He glanced around the room. One or two were nodding slightly. Others just sat still, unreadable.

Grace had leaned forward. Her hands remained loose in her lap, but her jaw was set.

"We appreciate the clarity, Clare. And the offer of trade."

A smile touched her lips, but didn't spread.

"But I always like to ask—when someone says *all our people are behind this*, who got to speak freely?"

It was Frank who spoke quickly, "We've taken great care with the transition, no one was forced. People saw the benefits. The decision to consolidate wasn't imposed—it was supported."

He glanced at Clare, then back to the room.

"We're not here to tell anyone how to live. But if there are ways we can support each other—through trade, shared infrastructure, even communication—we'd be foolish not to explore them."

Erik had been quiet until now. He spoke evenly, his gaze fixed on Frank.

"Thanks for coming. Your approach is interesting, and of course we're open to dialogue. But we've seen what happens when decisions only benefit one side—or certain people. We're not interested in dependencies or hierarchies."

His eyes moved to Clare.

"There have to be shared outcomes, and shared responsibilities. That's how we work here."

Harald felt like the room had been holding its communal breath. Now, chairs shifted and soft murmurs stirred as people leaned into low conversation.

Callum stood, rubbing a hand across his brow.

"You've given us something to think about, and we appreciate the visit. We'll take some time and talk things through—together."

People began filtering out of the hall, and Harald found himself near the stocky man from Nameth. The man had been silent through the entire meeting.

Outside, Harald caught the steady hum of the hydro installation. The stranger had noticed too—he was already moving toward it. Harald followed, and when the man turned, he finally spoke.

"Didn't realize you had this level of electrical generation," he said, eyeing the equipment. "Looks new?"

Harald glanced around, hoping to spot his father, but no one else seemed to have noticed the exchange. He hesitated, unsure how much to share, then settled on, "Yeah, we found it at another location. Relocated it here recently."

The man nodded, thoughtful. "I'm Ian. I handle tech on Nameth."

Harald extended a tentative hand. "Harald."

"Smart use of flow, Harald," Ian said, turning to rejoin the others. "Most people forget that water's still a kind of stored energy."

Harald was about to catch up with Lina and Cari when Bree stepped up beside him.

"The meeting went well," she said dryly. "Clare's speeches always make me feel like I've already agreed to something I haven't had time to really think about."

Harald glanced sideways. "Are you really all living together on one farm?"

"Yeah," Bree said. "It's a commune. Very efficient... the cult of Clare."

Cari had been waiting ahead. As they reached her, she gave Harald a questioning look—*What's going on?* Harald gave a small shake of his head, and the three of them continued down to the dock.

Up ahead, Callum and Frank walked with their heads together.

"Callum, it'd be great if we could get Jana over to Nameth—sooner rather than later," Frank said. His tone was friendly, but carried a subtle edge of insistence.

"Why don't you come too? We'll show you the progress we're making. Looks like it's going to be a bumper harvest this year."

The motorboat pulled away from the dock, the same way it arrived. Quietly powerful, a reminder of a past time that Talem had thought as faded and gone.

CHAPTER TWELVE

MARK PUSHED OFF from the bow of the old barge. He glanced back to Loretta, giving the signal to do the same at the stern. The river—dirty, slow-moving—would help them now. One direction only: downstream.

There was no going back. Not the way their parents had gone.

But the time for going back was over.

They had to move.

And downstream was the only way left.

Mark and Loretta each held a line, keeping the barge—*Drifter*—close to the bank. Not too far into the current. Just enough pull to keep it moving.

Lisa walked between them. She'd wanted to stay aboard, but Mark hadn't risked it. If the boat slipped the lines, they'd lose everything.

Better that she walked. Loretta could calm her when she protested.

They walked all day and saw no one.

When night fell, Mark and Loretta made fast to the bank. They ate a small meal—quiet, sparse. All three were bone tired.

They had covered maybe five miles.

By the next evening, they were nearing a town. They passed abandoned buildings—mostly commercial. Faded signs. Broken windows.

At last, they saw the first people.

Not many. Just a few. Watching.

They stood back as the children struggled with the barge.

Bearing witness. Neither helping nor hindering.

Mark found a place to tie up for the night.

He'd go into town tomorrow. Look for food.

Rest tonight.

Tomorrow would come—whether he wanted it to or not.

Loretta had wanted to join him. Said it made more sense to go together.

But Mark had shaken his head. Stay with Lisa. Safer that way, probably.

The town wasn't far. Mark walked with his hands in his pockets, shoulders pulled tight. His parents had done everything they could to keep them out of places like this.

Towns meant people. People meant risk.

The streets were quiet. Wind whistled through broken windows, hollowed buildings.

He saw them—people standing in doorways, moving slowly.

No one looked up. No waves. No nods.

The government building sat at the end of a wide, cracked parking lot. A limp flag marked its purpose.

Inside, a woman behind glass asked his name and checked his ID. She marked a ledger, then slid three small bags through the slot. Rice. Dry lentils. Flour.

Mark took them with quiet thanks.

He wondered if Loretta would've gotten more.

He wondered if *he* would have—if he'd had something to give. Something of value.

Not money. That was worthless now.

He wasn't even sure what counted as valuable anymore.

CHAPTER THIRTEEN

GRACE STOOD just inside the doorway, watching the usual rhythm of hands at work—a typical Study Hall morning. She listened to the buzz and fragments of speech unsurprised. Fuel reserves, shared living, abandoned farms. The motorboat's engine still rang faintly in everyone's mind.

Grace had been quietly shocked by the motorboat. Nameth must have fuel stored somewhere. Using it to arrive in Talem wasn't just transportation—it was a choice. A show of power, perhaps. Or maybe they simply needed to burn it before it went bad.

"Miss Grace?"

Jake's voice rose from the back of the room, gentle and questioning. "How come we don't have a motorboat?"

Grace paused, as all eyes in the room shifted her way.

"It's a good question, Jake. People used to have them here. But we knew the fuel wouldn't last. So we let them go."

The room stayed quiet.

"Nameth made a different choice. That doesn't make it wrong. But every decision brings its own consequences."

The room finally breathed but the questions kept coming.

"Could they really grow enough food for everybody on just one farm?" someone asked.

"Why do they have a Mayor? Does he make all the decisions?"

Grace faced them, their faces curious, unsettled, open.

"They've chosen efficiency," she said. "A single leader, common systems, communal living. It can work—especially in the short term. It's fast, and it's clear."

She let that settle, then added.

"Let's dig into some history."

Grace moved to her chair and settled in.

"We all need each other," she began. "Humans don't do well in isolation, and things work better when we get together. The whole is usually greater than the sum of the parts." She cast a glance around the room just to make sure they were still with her.

"Throughout history people have tried many ways to organize themselves. One way is to share everything, live together—to try and be equal. Once, they built a whole new country like this. Kibbutzim were places that grew food, they shared the labor and lived together. It's efficient and people work well with shared goals and outcomes."

It was Lina who was the first to ask, "But it doesn't always work, does it?"

Grace nodded, not surprised it came from Lina.

"No, it doesn't always work," the room was listening now.

"Often people start with good intentions, but over time shared purpose can begin to feel like pressure. Like control."

She looked down, searching her memories before going on.

"Systems like that can succeed for a while, but eventually their walls crack, or get torn down. It's true— we need each other. We are stronger together. But ignore the individual and it all begins to unravel."

Max spoke, his hand half raised, "So what do we do?" he asked. "If we see something wrong—how do we stop it?"

A murmur of agreement traveled the room.

Grace met his eyes, taking a second before she answered.

"You speak up," she said finally. "You ask hard questions. Even when it's uncomfortable. Especially then."

"And you make space—for difference and disagreement. That's how a community stays alive."

Erik stood just outside the Study Hall as Callum approached.

"There's a few people fired up in there," he said, tilting his head toward the door. "I suppose we ought to send someone over to Nameth—see what the fuss is really about."

Callum raised an eyebrow. "I'm guessing you think that someone is me?"

"You read my mind," Erik said, tapping his leg absently. "Take Jana. And bring Harald along, if he's willing."

Callum hesitated. "You sure about that? He's still a kid."

"Not anymore," Erik said quietly. "Not here. Not now."

They stood a moment, the breeze tugging gently at the grass.

"They must be farming hard to feed everyone off one plot," Callum said. "Pretty sure they've got a desal plant, too. That's a lot of power."

Erik nodded, gaze steady. "See what you find. Separate fact from fiction. That motorboat stunt was loud—but I'm not sure what they were really trying to prove."

Callum shrugged.

"Maybe they weren't trying to prove anything. Maybe they've just got things dialed in over there."

Erik didn't answer right away. His gaze lingered on the caldera that climbed up behind the town.

"Maybe," he said. "Or maybe they're running harder than they want to admit."

Callum gave a small nod, his expression uncertain.

"Guess we'll find out."

Erik caught up with Harald as he headed toward the workshop. Walking beside him, he lowered his voice.

"Harald, a quick word."

"We're sending a few people over to Nameth. I want you to go—with Callum and Jana."

Harald stopped, turning to face him.

"Are you sure I'm the right person?"

Erik placed a hand on his son's shoulder.

"Just watch. Listen. We'll talk when you're back."

He glanced toward the trail.

"You headed to the workshop?"

Harald adjusted the strap of his tool bag.

"Yeah."

"Same," Erik said, voice softening. "Meeting Lina. We're starting the hydro copy. You can lend a hand."

Harald and Lina spent the afternoon bent over the hydro schematics with their father. There was no space left for Nameth—only wiring diagrams, gear ratios, and scribbled notes.

They moved between sketches and salvaged parts, trying to decide if they could really build something so precise from what remained.

It was late afternoon when Harald remembered to swing by the radio room.

He pushed the door open and poked his head in.

Sarah waved him inside.

"Harald. I thought you might drop by. Nothing from Drifter today, if that's what you're looking for."

"I know you scan a lot of channels," he said, stepping closer. "It'd be easy to miss a weak transmission."

Sarah nodded, her tone calm but firm.

"He said he was moving the barge. His antenna could be blocked—or worse. There are plenty of reasons for silence."

She looked at him more closely now, the mood shifting.

"Harald... it's dangerous out there. You know that. His parents are likely gone. It's okay to care. But be careful how much you take on."

Harald didn't answer.

Sarah knew he was attached.

But she also knew he understood—like most of them did by now—that life beyond the island was a different kind of hard. Especially on the mainland.

Harald left Sarah and crossed the street toward the library. He'd promised to meet Cari there by day's end.

As he walked, hands in his pockets, his fingers turned over a few smooth pebbles he'd picked from a stream.

They weren't heavy—but they were still with him.

He thought about tossing them but didn't.

Maybe later.

Cari was sitting at a table in the middle of the room. It hadn't always been a library. Lina had told him—once—it was a summer tea room for visitors to the island.

Another age.

Harald imagined Cari, dressed in skirts, sipping tea from a delicate china tea cup. The thought was beginning to change his mood.

She hadn't heard him enter but somehow sensed him now. She smiled and motioned him to join her.

"You're just in time," she said, nodding to the book splayed open before her. "Apparently, every meal used to be a ceremony."

Harald pulled out a chair.

"Look at this," she said, pointing to the page. "They had something called a *fish course*. Not just fish for dinner—fish *as well* as dinner."

She flipped the heavy book around, tapping a diagram of an elaborate table layout.

"And between courses, you had to 'cleanse your palate' with sorbet."

She gave him a crooked grin.

"Can you imagine? Salad, fish, roast—and then a spoonful of icy fruit water just to reset. I think I'd need a nap before dessert."

Harald shook his head, the faintest smile forming.

"We're lucky to get two courses, both of them involving mushrooms."

"I'm heading to Nameth tomorrow," he added, the smile slipping. "Fact-finding mission with Callum and Jana."

"That should make Bree happy," Cari replied, a little too sharply. "She seemed pretty interested in getting close to you last time."

Harald paused. He found Bree faintly annoying—but the shift in Cari's tone landed. He moved a little closer.

"Well, there's probably an even chance they'll kidnap all of us and you'll never see me again. But if I *do* make it back..." He met her eyes. "I'm heading straight for you."

He leaned in. Their lips brushed, and she reached out, fingers finding his and threading them together.

Grace had slipped through the library door without either of them noticing, a stack of papers tucked firmly under one arm. Seeing Harald and Cari together, she allowed her boot to gently scuff the old wood floor.

They separated just in time to hear a quiet chuckle. "Looks like I've arrived at an important moment."

Harald straightened, and Cari adjusted the book.

"Don't worry," Grace's tone was reassuring. "This kind of thing happens all the time in libraries. Maybe it's the quiet, or more likely all the romantic stories that get people's hearts beating just a little faster."

She glanced between them—one with a warm flush rising, the other suddenly fascinated by the table.

Grace placed the stack of papers on their table and moved toward one of the shelves. "Harald," she said. "I know I told you to lose yourself in history with a sprinkle of philosophy. But in hindsight, I've been remiss."

She was walking back now with a small book cradled carefully with both hands. "I think you should read this."

She handed the book over and Harald read the title: *The Wizard of Earthsea. By Ursula K. LeGuin.*

The cover was worn but still clearly showed a dragon arcing over a dark sky.

"Books can teach us so much," Grace was smiling now. "But you don't find water in a dry well. Try this, hopefully it will help quench your thirst."

Her gaze moved to Cari. "Let me put some thought into a book for you. Don't worry, I'll find something."

"I was about your age when I first read that book," she said, returning to Harald. "But I didn't understand it then. Not really."

She looked between them, her voice steady but softened.

"It took losing a great deal to understand what it was trying to say."

Cari stilled. Harald looked up.

It was Cari who asked, though Harald had felt the question too.

"What was it?"

"What did you lose?"

"You know, I came to this island before it was called Talem. Summers mostly. But for many years, my home was the mainland—at the university. I lived for that place."

Grace folded her hands in her lap, fingers weaving and unweaving.

"I thought I had it all. A career. A life. A husband... a child."

Harald glanced at Cari, but she didn't look away from Grace.

"I loved history. I loved the rhythm of thought, the weight of ideas. But sometimes you make a choice—one that feels justified, even right—and later you understand it for what it really was."

Her voice didn't shake, but she drew a breath before continuing.

"I didn't come to the island out of hope. I came because I had nowhere else. I'd made a decision that cost me my family. My husband left, and he took our daughter. And I couldn't blame him."

Silence fell, but it didn't feel heavy—only honest.

"That was when I understood. What it means to have nothing. And to know you built the wreckage yourself."

She paused, eyes briefly on the window.

"I've never told that story to anyone here," she added, turning back to them. "But you two... you asked. And I guess I believe this place might give you the chance to live well. In some ways, better than we did."

Grace sat quietly for a moment, then turned to Harald. "I heard you're going to Nameth tomorrow."

He gave a small nod.

"They might live in ways that feel strange to you," she said. "But underneath all that... people are people. Don't forget that."

She rose, gathering her notes, then added more softly:

"Go with open eyes—and a steady heart."

Chapter Fourteen

Callum had taken the helm, while Harald managed the jib sheet on the old lugger. The onshore wind held steady at ten to twelve knots—just about perfect. As they cleared the harbor mouth, Callum raised the small mizzen. Ahead lay a couple of hours on a beam reach along Talem's coast, then another hour or so to cross over to Nameth.

Harald settled in, tucking a foot under the seat for balance. Lina sat beside him on the forward rail. It had been Jana's idea to bring her—she'd talked Erik into it. Lina was already helping with the stomach bug cases, and it made sense. She was learning more with every outing.

He looked west, out over the open water. Nearly five thousand miles of nothing in that direction—just wind and waves, and the slow curve of the planet. He wondered at the courage of the old-world mariners who had sailed off over other horizons without any certainty of arriving.

To starboard, the coast of Talem slipped by. Trees were growing lower down the cliffs than he remembered, stretching toward the spray—alder, spruce, and even a few sapling firs clawing for light. From the rocks, a heron lifted and glided inland. A trio of sea otters watched the lugger pass, then vanished with barely a splash.

Farther along the coast, remnants of the old world clung to a bluff. Holiday homes—once prized for their ocean views—were dissolving into the trees. Roofs slumped under the weight of moss. Decks had fallen away, scattered across the floor of the new forest. Non-native ivy still clawed at a few walls, but it was losing ground. Pacific blackberry had taken over—thick, thorny, relentless. The native vine was winning, draping collapsed porches and curling through broken windows, as if the land were reclaiming its own space.

Beyond the next rise, the cliffs gave way to the low, sheltered sweep of Wren Bay. The water lay calmer here— a slick mirror reflecting blue sky and dark pines. A scattering of seals were hauled out along the rocks, bodies touching as they dozed. One slid lazily into the shallows at the sight of the lugger.

Harald watched, beguiled by their beauty. He glanced toward the curve of the shoreline, where an old boathouse from the mansion days still stood. *What if we kept a boat here?* It would take half the time to cross from Talem. But he let the thought drop. Maybe they didn't want a quicker way to Nameth.

As they cleared the point, the coast fell away behind them. Open water now—nothing between them and their island neighbor but wind and sea. The breeze freshened— fifteen knots, maybe more—and the lugger responded.

Canvas strained, the hull heeled, spray whipping off the bow.

Harald grinned as the boat came alive beneath them. Across from him, Lina's face lit up, her hair flying wild. They'd make short work of the passage now. Nameth was already visible ahead, growing larger with every minute.

They were close when Callum spoke up over the wind.

"The harbor here's a bit tighter than Talem," he called to the crew. "Let's take it in on the jib."

Harald nodded and moved quickly to unclip the main halyard. At the stern, Jana did the same with the mizzen. Both sails dropped in a soft collapse. Harald gathered the canvas, tying it off clean as the lugger settled onto a steady keel. They were still making good way under jib alone.

The lugger slipped past the breakwater and into the narrow harbor.

The town looked deserted. Every building boarded or abandoned. Inside the harbor, there was no sign of the motorboat—or any other boat, for that matter. But as they neared the dock, a lone figure stood waiting. Callum brought them in with practiced ease. As they came alongside, smooth and quiet, Lina tossed a line up to Bree.

"You made good time," Bree said, tying the lugger off at the dock.

Callum answered, "Where's the mayor?"

"We didn't expect you so soon," Bree replied. "They're up at the farm. I'll take you."

Callum huffed, his irritation barely contained. But he jumped up to the dock and followed Bree, with Jana, Harald, and Lina trailing behind.

They followed Bree past shuttered windows and peeling paint. The street was silent, apart from the sea breeze whistling softly through broken eaves—a quiet, eerie backdrop.

Lina moved up beside Harald. "There's no one here," she said under her breath. "They weren't joking. They've completely abandoned the town—the port."

Harald felt it too. Why give up a place that could keep them connected? It made no sense.

The path wove inland before the buildings came into view. Harald noticed a shift in the land. The soil was tilled, the greens clustered in narrow rows—nothing wild growing. Ahead, rising from the slope, were metal frames stacked with trays: tight rows of lettuce and chard climbing upward, fed by a web of plastic piping.

Jana slowed, shading her eyes. "Vertical farming," she murmured. "No wonder they're so productive on a small plot like this."

Callum stopped, mouth slightly open. He spoke to no one in particular. "Wow. Who'd have thought of that."

They rounded the final bend. The main house stood ahead, ringed by a scatter of outbuildings. A man waited on the porch, arms crossed, eyes sharp. Callum stepped forward with the small basket.

"Apples from Talem," he said.

The man—Frank—cracked a smile. "We gave up on trees. Too much space, too long to yield. But I won't say no to something that smells like sun."

Frank stepped down from the porch as Callum handed him the basket. He glanced at each of them in turn, then said, "Apologies for not meeting you at the dock. We weren't expecting you so soon. I hope Bree gave a warm welcome."

He held up the apples, then nodded. "Let's find Clare, and we'll take you on a quick tour."

Clare stepped out from one of the outbuildings as they approached, wiping her hands on a rag. She extended her hand—Callum first, then Jana—with practiced ease. She gave the children a quick smile, more reflex than warmth, then turned to lead them on.

Clare's enthusiasm as they approached the vertical growing racks surprised them. She had been sharp and efficient during her presentation on Talem. Now she beamed as she described the crops and the growing process.

"We've managed to get five full tiers running now. Greens mostly—lettuce, chard, mustard, kale. A few herbs. Minimal soil, drip-fed nutrients. We can grow year-round with a little light management."

Jana nodded, studying the setup. "How do you circulate nutrients?"

"Filtered compost tea, mostly," Clare said, clearly enjoying the question. "We've got a sealed system—nothing lost."

"And the trays? Did you salvage or fabricate?"

"A mix. Old storage bins, cut to size. A few we had to cast."

Jana squinted toward the horizon, where the sea shimmered faintly beyond the fields.

"And the water?"

Frank stepped up beside them. "Desal. Solar-powered. Pulling from a few hundred yards offshore."

Callum let out a short whistle.

Jana didn't respond right away. Her gaze stayed fixed on the coastline.

Frank glanced at Jana, misreading her silence. "It's a good system," he said, his tone warming.

Took some work to get right, but it's stable. Sustainable. Scalable"

Callum nodded, clearly impressed. "Looks like the future."

Jana said nothing. Her arms were crossed now, eyes still on the sea.

Harald watched her, then looked to Frank, to the neat rows of trays and plastic piping, the flat terrain fenced tight with efficiency. Everything ordered. Nothing left to chance.

If this was the future, he thought, *what had they done with the rest of it?*

As the conversation trailed off, Bree appeared at Lina's side and slipped her hand into hers. "Come on," she said brightly. "You're staying tonight, right? Dinner's already in the works. Let me show you where we all live."

Lina glanced at Harald, then back at Bree. "Sure."

They turned off the main path, passing between outbuildings, their voices fading into the hum of the compound.

Frank touched Callum on the elbow. "Great idea. Let's move the tour back to the farm. I think you'll like what you see."

Bree led Lina through a covered walkway to a cluster of squat stone outbuildings. "They picked this farm because of all the buildings. We can all live on-site." Her grip on Lina's hand relaxed as they stepped inside.

"These are our bunks," she said. "The young people sleep here."

Lina looked around. The room was clean and orderly—stacked bedding on unused beds, shared storage bins lining the walls.

"You and Harald can sleep in here tonight," Bree said, pointing to a vacant set of bunks. "It'll be fun to have a friend over."

Back at the vertical racks, Frank gestured toward a low structure lined with solar panels.

"Power station's there. Battery bank inside. Water treatment adjacent. We've modeled it to scale up or replicate."

Jana tilted her head. "How many people can you house?"

"Right now? Fifty, maybe a few more. We could stretch to sixty, and build out if needed. There's an adjacent farm we could bring online."

"And if you outgrow even that?"

Frank paused. "Then we build again. Somewhere else, if we have to. The model is set up for expansion."

They moved toward the farm buildings next. Harald found himself wishing he'd gone with Lina and Bree. The place seemed perfectly organized—power, water, food, housing. Everything with a place. And yet, something about it left him unsettled.

He glanced at Jana. She was quiet now, walking a step behind the others, her eyes flicking over the details—solar inverters, drainage trenches, the angle of the grow lights inside the sheds. She didn't say anything, but Harald could feel it: she was seeing what he couldn't name yet.

As they neared the main farm buildings, a group of residents came into view—four or five of them walking up from the lower field, sleeves rolled, hands dusty. They were laughing about something, one of them still mid-story.

"Hey there," one called as they passed, offering a wave.

"Welcome," another added, smiling as they moved on toward the outbuildings.

Harald gave a nod in return. They seemed... fine. Relaxed, even. Life on Nameth was different. He knew Erik would want to understand why—and how. Harald wasn't sure he'd be able to explain it.

Dinner was served outside—fifty people seated at long tables under solar-powered string lights. Frank spoke to Callum, who was seated to his right.

"We can eat inside—it's a squeeze—but while summer lasts, this is where we'd rather be."

Lina and Bree had their heads together. Harald caught fragments of their conversation.

"The dorms are fun."

"Lewis snores."

"I miss my own room."

He wondered what it would be like to share a bedroom with twenty other people—and guessed tonight he'd find out.

There was a buzz at dinner, fifty people eating and talking all at once. Clare leaned in to Jana.

"I know you're making it work on Talem. But what we have here... it could work on Talem too. We could help you get there—with a little guidance."

Harald hadn't heard the words, and Jana's face gave nothing away. But he noticed her fingers, gripping her knife and fork—knuckles turning white.

Dinner broke up slowly, people fading into the compound in twos and threes. Some stayed behind for cleanup; others drifted toward the dorms or the path beyond the outbuildings.

Harald found himself among the washing-up crew, stacking plates beside a boy about his age with short hair and a sunburned nose.

"First time here?" the boy asked.

"Yeah."

"It's not bad. Quiet in the mornings. Warm showers if you're early."

Harald nodded. Warm showers—he'd like to try that. "Thanks."

They worked in silence after that, hands moving over warm water and chipped enamel bowls. It felt normal enough.

Later, in the dormitory, Lina climbed into the top bunk. She leaned over the edge and whispered, "Tell me if you feel strange in the middle of the night. I don't know why, but I might wake up weird."

Harald stared at the bottom of her bunk for a while after that, waiting for sleep.

The dorm was still in half-light when Harald opened his eyes. The sounds of sleeping and the shapes of beds and bodies were just beginning to sharpen in the early morning gloom.

He slipped out of his bunk. Lina's above him was already empty.

Outside, the sky was shifting from charcoal to blue, and a faint breeze stirred the tops of the trees. He spotted two figures by the water shed—Jana crouched, Lina standing nearby, holding a field notebook.

He crossed the gravel to meet them.

Jana glanced up. "Up early."

"Yeah."

She returned to her work, unscrewing a vial and holding it under the spigot's flow. "We'll bring these back to the lab. I want to look at everything—bacteria, trace metals, get a baseline."

Lina looked at the notebook. "I'm recording time and source."

"Perfect, Lina." Jana stood, ready to move to the next sample. "Let's get this wrapped up. I don't know about you, but I'm ready to head home."

They approached Frank, who was standing with Clare and Callum near the porch of the old farmhouse.

"Frank, I got the samples," Jana said, stepping ahead of Lina. "We'll run them under the scope and I'll tabulate the results—get back to you, probably next week."

"Thanks, Jana," Frank said with a smile—still the gracious host. "I hope you all enjoyed yourselves. We'd love to hear what the folks on Talem think about our setup. We think it makes a lot of sense, given the way things are."

Callum extended a hand. "We appreciate it. Hope we can get together again soon—it's comforting to have such good neighbors so close."

They turned from the farm and began the walk back to the dock.

As they picked their way down the hill, Jana touched Callum's shoulder. "Let's take the east coast route back. I know it's a little longer, but there are a couple of things I want to look at."

Callum shrugged. "That's fine. With the early start, we've got plenty of time."

They sailed out of the harbor under a low morning sky, the wind lighter than the day before but steady enough. The lugger moved well, sails pulling gently, the island falling away behind them.

Jana stood near the bow, eyes scanning the coastline.

"Looking for something?" Harald asked.

"Just curious where the desal intake is," she said. "Should be out a couple hundred yards. Might be marked."

He followed her gaze. The shoreline was quiet, the compound already shrinking into the bluff. Farther out, a faint bob of red plastic moved with the swell.

"Could be that," she murmured.

They passed the marker Jana had guessed was tied to the desal intake—two or three hundred yards offshore, beyond the shallows. Nothing obvious, just a red buoy and a faint distortion in the water's surface. Harald watched her studying it, saying nothing.

Ten minutes later, as they curved along the east coast, the smell hit first. Faint at first, then stronger.

Jana moved to the rail, eyes narrowing. "Slow up a second."

Callum eased the mainsail, and Harald released the jib sheet. The lugger lost speed, coasting now.

Off the starboard side, the water took on a milky sheen. Not wide, but unnatural—oily, with a faint yellow tinge that caught the light. Near the rocks, a froth had gathered where a pipe met the surf.

"Oh no," Jana muttered. "That's sewage. That's not runoff. That's raw."

No one spoke. The sea made its usual sounds, unchanged, indifferent.

"We should head back," Callum said quietly. "Let them know about it."

Jana's gaze moved from Lina to Harald, then settled on Callum. "Oh, I think they already know about it."

CHAPTER FIFTEEN

THE QUIET IN THE BOAT was palpable, each of them lost in thought. They got the vessel moving again, steering down the east side of the island—the mainland-facing coast.

You could see the mainland from Highpoint on a clear day, but down here on the water, it was over the horizon.

Harald's gaze drifted inland. Most of Talem's farms had been built along this edge, sheltered from the worst of the weather in a way the western coast never was. Things had just evolved that way. Not all the farms were still running now, but even the ones left idle had held up. It was different on the west side.

Callum who broke the silence first.

"They probably just repurposed an old outflow," he said, not looking at anyone in particular. "That's how it used to work on these islands. Discharge lines straight to the sea."

No one answered.

He went on, more to himself now. "It's not new. We lived like that before. For years. It's no different, really."

Harald looked at Jana. She wasn't going to get pulled into this discussion. Sensibly, Harald thought, she would let him work this one out with himself.

Surprisingly, it was Lina who spoke.

"It *is* different," she said. "Back then we didn't know better. Now we do."

Callum glanced at her. He swallowed like he was about to argue. But he didn't.

Harald dropped a hand into the water, letting the boat's motion pull it along. The coolness climbed to his forearm—a grounding kind of cold.

He tried to shape the visit into a report for his father.

They're growing a lot of food. People seem happy. They eat well. Dormitories are strange, but we share space too—like the workshop.

But then there was the sewage.

What was that? Out of sight, out of mind?

The dock finally came into view around the headland—Talem's familiar shape against the darkening sea.

Callum was at the helm. He didn't say anything, didn't call for sail drop or adjust the sheets. Just kept the lugger on course, the wind full and trimmed in her canvas.

Harald opened his mouth to ask, "Shall we..."

But Callum wasn't listening.

The dock steaming toward them, the boat sliced clean and fast through the harbor mouth.

At the last possible moment, he pushed the tiller hard and swung the bow violently into the wind. The sails snapped, caught, luffed wildly. The hull rocked, slowed, coasted sideways.

And stopped.

They were alongside the dock, with Erik taking the line. "What was all that about," he asked. His face registering a complete lack of comprehension.

Erik's eyes moved to Jana and Lina. "Shall we schedule a meeting?"

"That's a good idea," Jana said, already stepping off the still-bobbing lugger. "Let's do it this evening. I'm going to borrow your daughter first—bit of lab work to sort through."

As they moved onto the dock, Cari was waiting. She stepped forward, eyes on Harald. She didn't speak, but the question was there—clear in her expression.

Well?

Harald looked at her, unsure where to start. He gave the faintest shake of his head—not no, not exactly, but not simple either.

"We'll talk later," he said quietly. Then he turned and followed Erik up the path.

Jana walked into the clinic, dropped her satchel beside the bench, and stood for a moment without saying anything.

"You're back," Hamish said, stating the obvious—a habit Jana knew well.

"We are," she replied. She didn't sit.

Hamish looked up. "It's bad?"

She hesitated. "Not catastrophic. Yet."

He raised an eyebrow, waited.

She exhaled. "Once you get past the cult vibe they're cultivating, you mean?"

Hamish raised the other eyebrow.

"They're compacting too many people, pushing their systems too hard. Their water management is crude. I've seen better containment in camp toilets."

"That doesn't surprise me," Hamish said. "But I wasn't sure you were going to say it out loud."

"I wasn't either."

He smiled—just a little. "Feels good, though, doesn't it?"

Jana didn't answer. She opened a cupboard and began pulling out slides, lining them up on the bench.

"Lina?" she called.

"Right here," came a voice from the hallway. Lina stepped in, sleeves already rolled, hair pulled back.

Lina and Jana worked steadily, shoulder to shoulder at the long bench. Slides were stained and sealed, water samples spun down in the centrifuge, algae counts tallied under the scope. Jana moved with the practiced precision of someone who had done this a hundred times. Lina was slower, but careful, following the work carefully.

By late afternoon, the last slide was under the microscope. Jana adjusted the focus with her thumb, made a soft sound in her throat—half acknowledgment, half concern.

Hamish glanced over from the counter. "What've you got?"

She sat back, pulling off her gloves. "The coastal water near the desal draw is showing elevated bacterial markers. Still below illness threshold, but just. It's consistent with light fecal contamination."

Lina frowned. "From the outflow?"

Jana shook her head. "I didn't sample the outflow. I know what's there—I could smell it from the boat. This was from the intake pipe near the desal. If that's being touched by the same water..."

Hamish leaned in. "Tide wash?"

"Maybe. They're probably still using an old discharge line from when the ferry terminal had a full septic system. But that was designed for a different sea level. With the ocean creeping higher and the tides coming in stronger, I think it's pushing back into the intake zone. The dilution's not carrying the waste far enough anymore."

Lina looked up from the bench. "So what does that mean?"

"It means the system works—until it doesn't. And no one seems to be watching the tide tables."

She paused, then added, "Also—there's something off in their nutrient loop. I pulled a sample from the feed reservoir under the vertical racks. It's cloudy. High nitrates. A few things growing that shouldn't be."

Hamish raised a brow. "You think it is impacting their produce?"

"Well," she said, "With what we just found, I don't think anyone should be eating the greens without boiling them first."

The hall filled quickly. Word had spread. Even the older residents who rarely left their porches found a seat. Children sat cross-legged along the back wall. Jake was bouncing a rubber ball against the plaster and plucking it from the air.

Erik stood near the front—not elevated, but central, as he always was. He waited until the last murmurs faded, then cleared his throat.

"We're grateful to the crew who made the crossing," he said. "Many of you were here for the meeting when the Nameth folk visited. You've probably heard pieces of this trip over there. Let's try and make some sense of it tonight."

He glanced to his right.

"Callum, go ahead."

Callum stood from the bench, hands resting on his thighs. He didn't pace or gesture—just spoke.

"They've made progress," he began. "Food's abundant. Spirits are high. There's order, if not structure. Most work in groups—shared duties, shared spaces."

He paused, weighing the words.

"It's different," he said. "But it's working. For now."

There was a beat of silence. Then Erik turned.

"Jana?"

She stepped forward, a folded page in one hand, a sample jar in the other. Her voice was calm.

"We took water samples from three points around Nameth," she said. "The intake near the desal plant showed elevated bacterial markers. Still below illness threshold—but only just. It's consistent with low-level fecal contamination."

She let that settle. Then continued.

"I also pulled a sample from the nutrient stream feeding their vertical grow system. High nitrate levels. Cloudy profile. Algal signatures in a closed loop. Whatever they're using for filtration—it's not catching everything."

A murmur passed through the room. She raised the jar slightly.

"But there's a larger issue," she said. "We observed raw sewage being discharged directly into the ocean, southeast of the settlement."

The calm shattered.

Chairs scraped. People stood, voices rising in alarm. Shouts carried across the room—What does that mean? What can we do?

Erik waited, arms folded, until the noise began to fall back.

"Let Jana finish."

She took a breath.

"It's definitely a smoking gun. It's likely the reason the Conways had stomach trouble." She paused. "The problem is, their waste system isn't engineered. It's inherited—an old discharge pipe, designed for another time. Another climate. It's failing. Slowly, maybe. But it's failing."

Sarah was still standing after Jana had finished. "We need to tell them to stop polluting. This is unacceptable. Erik? Grace? What are we going to do?"

Grace stood slowly, unfolding herself like someone surfacing from deeper thought. She didn't raise her voice—she never did—but the meeting waited, holding their breath.

"They're trying to make the system fit the results they want," she said. "But the world doesn't work like that."

She stepped forward, hands loosely clasped in front of her.

"Their system wasn't designed by engineers. That's not the problem. Ours wasn't either. The problem is when you stop looking—when you stop asking what your choices are doing to the land, the water, and the people downstream."

She glanced toward Jana.

"We can tell them. And maybe they'll listen. Or maybe they'll say we're judging them. But either way, the ocean will keep telling the truth."

Erik stepped in smoothly, quick to follow her thoughts.

"Let's work on a radio transmission," he said. "We'll wrap the sewage outflow into Jana's report, keep it clear and respectful."

He paused, then added, "Suggestions. Not orders."

The meeting ended, but no one left right away. People stood in small clusters, voices low and thoughtful. The air felt thicker somehow.

Outside, the last of the evening light streaked the sky. Erik was speaking quietly with Grace near the doorway when Peter approached.

"We can't keep doing this," Peter said. "The sprint up to Highpoint, the patchy signal—we need a better way to communicate."

Erik nodded slowly. "We've talked about it. Maybe it's time to make something more permanent."

"Well, now seems like a good time."

Harald had been nearby, listening without meaning to. He stepped forward. "We might have what we need. There's an old repeater rig in Supply—tagged for the fire network, pre-collapse. We can power it with a small battery and a solar setup. The hardest part would be hauling it up to Highpoint."

Erik gave a single nod. "Bring Tommy in on it. If it looks workable, let's do it."

Harald had liked the hikes to Highpoint, but this would make the well checks easier. And it improved their link to Nameth.

It took a couple of days to rig the repeater. The frame had rusted, and some of the wiring needed replacing, but the bones were still solid. Harald and Tommy lashed the unit to a salvaged pack frame, took turns with the weight, and reached the summit just before dusk. They bolted it to the old watchtower and left the panel tilted south for maximum sun exposure.

Back in the radio room the next morning, Harald powered up the base unit and switched to UHF. He ran a quick test loop, then keyed the mic.

"Nameth Station, this is Talem Radio. Do you read us? Repeat—Nameth, this is Talem. Testing repeater relay from Highpoint. Over."

There was a pause, a soft crackle—and then a voice came through, clearer than Harald had ever heard.

"Talem, this is Nameth Station. Reading you loud and clear. Solid five by five. That's a beautiful signal. Over."

He smiled, then thumbed the mic again.

"Copy that, Nameth. Relay appears stable. Let's keep this frequency open for daily check-ins at 0900. Thanks for the return. Over and out."

Harald leaned back in the chair, the quiet around him sharper now with that new thread of connection. For the first time in months, the silence felt slightly less complete.

Erik and Grace had composed a message for Nameth—scheduled as the first formal transmission at nine. It included Jana's lab report and a clear, respectful request: to cease discharging waste into the shared ocean waters.

Harald checked the wall clock. Still a few minutes to go.

He stayed seated as Sarah stepped into the room, carrying a folded page and a thermos of tea. She nodded to him as she settled behind the mic.

"Thanks for warming the seat," she said, her voice dry but kind.

At exactly 0900, Sarah keyed the mic.

"Nameth Station, this is Talem Radio with a formal message. Please advise if ready to receive. Over."

A pause, then: "Talem, this is Nameth. Go ahead. Over."

Sarah unfolded the paper and read, her tone steady and unflinching.

"This is a transmission on behalf of the Talem community. We are grateful for continued communication and mutual aid. During a recent visit, water samples were taken from three sites around your settlement. The intake near the desalination plant showed elevated bacterial markers consistent with low-level fecal contamination. We also observed untreated discharge entering the sea south of your harbor. These findings suggest possible tide wash affecting your intake zone."

She paused, letting that settle.

"We share these observations not as judgment, but as concern. We're all adapting to a changing world. The ocean doesn't keep secrets. Respectfully, we recommend ceasing discharge and reviewing intake placement. Lab findings are available if helpful. Talem Radio out."

She let go of the mic and exhaled slowly.

The radio hissed quietly for a moment, then a voice returned.

"Copy all, Talem. Message received. Appreciate the clarity. We'll review with the mayor. Nameth out."

Sarah leaned back in her chair. "Well," she said, half to herself, "that's either the beginning of something good— or something else entirely."

Harald didn't answer. He just listened to the hum of the equipment and the faint crackle of the open channel, as if something more might come.

CHAPTER SIXTEEN

MARK HAD THE MAPBOOK laid out on the small dining table of the barge. Rand McNally—not exactly a river chart, but good enough to track the towns they'd passed. And the ones still ahead.

After the first town, they'd kept moving. Manhandling the boat with lines from the riverbank—one step at a time, inching the barge downstream. Even Lisa was helping now.

Sometimes it got tricky. Trees reached right to the waterline. Roots tangled in the mud. They worked as a team to keep the lines from snagging—or worse, dropping into the slow-moving river.

The poles had been Lisa's idea.

"What if we pushed the barge instead?" she'd asked. "Like in Venice."

They kept close to the bank. Once, when the water ran too deep for the poles, Mark had jumped in and hauled the barge toward shore with a line clenched in his fist.

It was less work that way—staying off the bank kept them out of reach of the strangers they sometimes glimpsed at the river's edge.

Food wasn't plentiful, but most days their stomachs weren't empty. They boiled rice when they had it, added what they could forage, or used the dry beans from the government store. It wasn't enough to grow on, but it was enough to keep going.

The girls were leaner now, but not frail. Loretta kept a record of their meals in a weathered notebook—dates, quantities, careful notes in small handwriting. Lisa filled the margins with sketches: the river, the trees, the animals they sometimes saw.

They came to a town with a different feel. At the landing, after they'd tied up, two men were waiting. They asked a few questions—where they'd come from, how many aboard, what they needed—then waved them through. The tone was wary, not hostile.

Inside, the place had energy. Not order, but effort. People trying to make it work.

The government store still opened on certain days, and this one had cheese. Someone had set up a second shop beside it—a kind of sharing shelf, where extra goods changed hands without currency.

Bread was baking somewhere. The smell reached them before the loaves did. Someone passed pieces to the girls— no ID, no names, just warmth given freely..

For a moment, they thought they could stay.

They did stay—a couple of days. No one bothered them, and the girls got warm bread again the next morning. Mark helped unload a shipment at the dock and traded for a tin of lentils. Loretta was given a coat that almost fit.

On the third day, a woman from the supply office came to the barge. She was polite, almost apologetic. There just wasn't room, she said—not for the long term. They'd had to turn others away too.

She wished them luck. Said a few places downriver were doing okay. Maybe even better than here.

They weren't being forced out. Not exactly. But they couldn't stay.

They'd kept moving. But as they approached the next town, Mark saw the dock was blocked with barbed wire. A painted X marked a building near the waterline.

It was getting late, but somehow he managed to get the barge across to the other bank. They drifted downriver a while, then moored against a stand of trees.

In the morning, a woman approached from the far side—alone in a small rowboat. She didn't come close, just hailed them across the water.

Stay away.

Cholera.

Half the town was dead or dying.

They kept going.

That evening, they sat quietly on the barge, just beyond a bend where the water slowed and the sounds of the river fell away.

They had talked about this life. A life without hope.

Mark opened the mapbook again. The pages were soft at the edges, creased and stained. He traced the faded lines with a finger—the river winding like thread through towns that might or might not still exist. They were close now. Close to the coast.

Close to the island.

He rose and crossed to the shortwave. He hadn't touched it in days. The airwaves had been filled with stories like theirs—same losses, different voices.

But now they were closer. The island. The boy, Harald.

Mark adjusted the frequency.

And picked up the handset.

CHAPTER SEVENTEEN

SARAH WAS ABOUT to shut down the shortwave for the night. Different day, same stories floating across the static—crackling voices from somewhere out there, each one a scrap of a fading world. They'd talked about cutting back, maybe monitoring just a few hours a day. But the signal, faint as it was, still mattered to Sarah. As long as someone was reaching out, Talem wasn't alone.

She reached for the switch, fingers grazing the toggle—when the radio crackled. Sharp and close. This wasn't a background hiss or some faint echo of an emergency broadcast. Sarah leaned forward and turned up the gain. There was a quick burst and a thin voice buried deep in the noise. ".... This is Drifter... is anyone listening?"

Sarah grabbed a pen and paper. This message was going to travel—not sit in the radio room log.

"Go ahead, Drifter," she said. "This is Island Station."

She logged the conversation as it came, then paused to read it back. Satisfied, she tore the page from her notebook, folded it into her jacket pocket, and stood.

Erik and the kids were going to want to hear this.

Sarah arrived breathless. Erik, Harald, and Lina were at the kitchen table—peeling root vegetables, Harald stirring a sizzling pot.

It was Erik who spoke. "You look like you've seen a ghost," he quipped. "Or, more likely, heard one."

Sarah didn't smile. She held up the folded page.

"Shortwave. Just now. It was Drifter—Mark. They all made it down river. All of them. He's close to the coast. He asked for our coordinates." Sarah paused to catch her breath. "They're looking for somewhere safe."

The kitchen quieted. Even the pot on the stove seemed to fall back to a softer simmer.

Harald had turned from the stove. He knew protocol. They never gave out their location. It wasn't safe.

Erik rose from his seat now. "And what did you say?"

Sarah met his eyes. "I said I'd pass the message along. That's all."

He gave a single nod, not of approval or judgment— just acknowledgement.

Lina spoke next, quiet but firm. "So what do we do?"

No one answered right away. The steam rose from the pot. A spoon rested in Harald's hand, unmoving. Outside, a gull called once and was gone.

Harald broke the silence. "He's smart. Careful. The way he spoke, the way he waited. He's been listening. Probably knows more than he says."

Sarah nodded. "He mentioned the coast. He's been using a Rand McNally to log his progress."

"Rand McNally," Erik said, already at the bookshelf, pulling an old road atlas from between two weathered volumes. "I think I have an idea. These maps are broken into grids"

Harald joined him. "We can use the grid references to communicate locations. That's brilliant."

Erik had the mapbook open now to the mainland coast, tracing one of the rivers with his finger until it met the ocean. "Sarah, you're pretty sure they came down this river?"

She stepped closer. "Yes. That's the one."

"That's a good stretch south of us," Harald said, leaning in. "A couple days' walk at least, maybe more, if they follow the shoreline."

Lina had been quiet until now. But her voice cut through the room with conviction.

"There's only one way to make sure," she said.

They all turned toward her.

"We have to go and get them."

Harald accompanied Sarah back to the radio room. A short message. Drifter was waiting.

Harald keyed the mic. "Drifter, come in. This is Island Station."

"Copy that, Island Station."

"You'll need to stand by until tomorrow for coordinates. Hold on to that road atlas. Station out."

The meeting wasn't formally called, but early the next morning most of the core families had gathered in the town hall. Word moved fast on Talem—especially when it carried the shape of a decision.

Erik stood at the front, with Grace and Callum nearby. Sarah gave a brief account of the shortwave exchange—how Drifter had identified himself as Mark, confirmed his sisters were alive, and requested coordinates. She left out the hesitation in his voice, but those who knew her could read it anyway.

No vote was taken. But there was discussion. Quiet, serious. A few voiced concern about exposure—reminding the room that Talem's strength was its silence. Others, mostly older, reminded them of the early days, when boats came from the mainland not with strangers but with cousins, with friends. With hope.

It wasn't unanimous, but there was a movement toward yes.

Erik offered no speech, just the weight of his presence. Callum would go. They would prep the lugger. They would confirm coordinates and time for a pickup. A tight window. If the passengers were not there, they would abort. A mission that would only sail when there was the best chance to succeed.

People lingered afterward, some moving in small circles, others moving off to start their day.

And then Peter stepped in from the radio room, out of breath.

"There's a message," he said. "From Nameth."

It had been days since Sarah's carefully worded message advising of the lab results, and Talem's concern of raw sewage discharging into their shared waters.

Callum spoke first. "Peter, what did they say?"

Peter carefully opened the logbook to today's date. "I wrote it down... word for word."

The townspeople quieted, giving Peter a moment to calm himself.

Peter ran a hand through his hair and glanced down at the page. His voice steadied.

"Nameth acknowledges receipt. The matter is under review. That was the phrase: 'under review.'"

Grace and Erik exchanged a glance but waited for Peter to continue.

"We are monitoring all systems and will review internally. At this time, we request that you refrain from further communication or accusations."

A low murmur swept through the hall. Erik's face was unchanged, but a ripple touched his jaw as he ground his teeth. Callum let out a breath he'd been holding. Grace's eyes narrowed.

"That sounds like a threat," Cari said, stepping forward. "What can we do now?"

It was Jana who moved next, making her way to the front.

"This isn't a surprise," she said quietly. "There's no doubt they feel entitled to farm the way they choose. Live the way they choose. Any fallout from that is our problem, not theirs."

Erik nodded. "I think our options are limited for now. Jana, let's reach out to all the east-side farms—no harvesting seaweed or shellfish. The best we can do right now is protect ourselves."

Peter hadn't moved, but he spoke again, eyes still on the page.

"There's one more thing. The message wasn't from Mayor Wells. It was from Clare Drew."

A silence followed—not the shocked kind, but slower, more thoughtful.

Harald felt it sit.

Clare. Not Wells.

He glanced toward Erik, then Grace, but neither of them spoke. It wasn't just who sent the message—it was what it implied. That Wells was stepping back, or being pushed aside. That Clare was the voice now.

Was she running things?

Harald didn't know what it meant, not exactly. But Clare wasn't just speaking for Nameth—she was steering it.

The room cleared slowly, voices trailing as people drifted outside. Grace and Jana were deep in conversation. Grace suggested it would be useful to document the situation on Nameth. Jana agreed to write a report with the lab findings, but also the social and work structures at the commune.

Erik pulled Harald aside. "We need to talk about the mainland trip."

"We can leave in a few days," Harald said. "I'll radio Drifter and establish coordinates for the pickup."

"Yes, let's work on the exact location," Erik said, turning to face him. "But Callum and Peter will be making the trip."

Harald blinked. "Why?"

"They've both sailed that route before. They know the currents, and they've worked together under pressure."

"I've trained on that boat," Harald said. "I made contact. I can do this."

"I know," Erik said. "And I'm proud of you for that."

He paused, measuring the next words.

"But if something happens out there—if the kids don't show, or the boat's in danger—I need someone who can make the call to turn back. Without hesitation."

Harald's jaw tightened. "You don't think I could do that."

"I think you care Harald, but this is dangerous. I'm not sure you could make a decision to leave them. Even if that was the right one."

They stood in silence for a beat. Harald's shoulders stiffened, then he gave a small nod—tight and unreadable.

"Okay," he said.

He stepped past Erik and out into the light. The breeze was strengthening, coming off the water sharp and heavy.

By late afternoon, the wind was blowing. Thirty knots, maybe more. Gusting—gale force seven, edging toward eight.

Harald made his way to the dock, eyes on the bay, watching whitecaps whip across the surface. A wind flag stood rigid, snapping and cracking in the gusts. The boats rocked against their lines, hulls groaning.

He didn't hear her approach, but then Cari was there, falling into step beside him as he reached the beached lasers.

"What are you planning?" she asked as he pulled a sail bag and PFD from the beach locker.

Harald inclined his head toward the chop. "Thought it might be fun to blow off some steam."

Cari followed his gaze, but it was Harald who spoke again, "You're welcome to come. It might not be totally... safe."

Cari grinned. "I'm not totally in love with safe." She pulled her own life jacket from the locker.

"Let's take one boat," Harald said. "I'll helm."

They rigged the Laser together, silent and practiced. Cari double-checked the downhaul tension while Harald clipped in the rudder and gave the daggerboard one last shove.

They launched fast from the beach—Harald pushing off, then jumping in to grab the tiller and mainsheet. Cari shifted to balance the Laser as it caught the wind and heeled hard.

Harald pointed the boat out into the bay. The gale carrying them fast. The sea broke over bow and rail, soaking them. The wind flashing across their faces lighting them with the thrill of it. Their feet locked in the toe straps, bodies working to keep the boat level. Harald held the position on the wind. Sailing hard and tight.

They barely spoke. Words were meaningless. Their bodies did the talking—reading gusts, adjusting weight with a shift of the hips, an arch of the back.

At the far end of the bay, Harald pushed hard on the tiller, tacking them tight upwind. Cari grunted as she moved across the boat, hair slick with spray, eyes flashing. She was inches from him, their shoulders brushing.

"We're not bad in storms," she said over the wind.

He glanced at her, smiling—breathless—-alive.

They tacked again and let the wind carry them back toward shore on a broad reach. As they rounded the lee point, the gusts eased. Harald loosed the mainsail, letting it flap. The boat rocked, catching its breath.

Up on the headland, a figure watched—then turned.

Grace walked back toward town.

Nameth could be Nameth.

And Talem would be Talem.

CHAPTER EIGHTEEN

THE MAPBOOK lay open on the table, its cover curled and worn. Callum, Erik, and Harald studied the coast. The river opened to the ocean miles south of Talem.

"Best-case scenario," Callum said, pointing directly across from the island. "We sail straight over, pick up the kids, and head straight back. Two hours to get there, so four hours round trip."

Erik and Harald looked at the route. Straightforward. Safe for the lugger, assuming fair wind.

They hadn't noticed Lina join them, but now she raised a hand and pointed.

"There's a grid line intersect just north of the river. That would be the best place to get them."

Harald followed her finger. She was right. A beach sat right there—no houses, no confusion. Mark couldn't mistake a pick-up point if it landed square on a grid line.

Callum had followed her finger too. "Lina, that's fifteen miles south. We'd be sailing five hours just to get there. Longer if the wind or tide turns."

"You're right," Lina said. She had their full attention now. "But with your pick-up zone, three people have to walk the same fifteen miles—one of them a child. Even at a good pace, they won't make it in a day. And they'd have to pass all this." She ran her finger along the map, over the dots marking coastal towns. "Who knows what's going on there."

Erik's hand landed on Callum's shoulder. "She's right. They're exposed if they try to walk it. Too many unknowns on that road."

His grip tightened. "But the risk shifts to you. I won't send you unless you're certain."

Callum turned to Lina. Her expression gave nothing away, but she didn't look down. He nodded once, "We can do it. We'll get an early start—back in time for dinner, most likely."

Harald clicked the mic as the sun cleared the ridge, the radio room feeling tighter than usual with the others standing by.

"Drifter, this is Island Station. Do you copy?"

There was a long silence—then a burst of static. The voice came through faint, distant.

"...Island Station, this is Drifter. Copy. Expected your call yesterday... is everything... alright?"

"Change of plan, Drifter. No coordinates over the air." Harald exhaled sharply. "We are coming for you."

He waited a beat, then continued. "Do you have a usable handheld—walkie-talkie?"

"Yeah," Mark said. "It'll hold a charge for a few hours."

"Good," Harald said. "There's a beach just north of your river—falls right on a grid line. No houses. We need you there tomorrow. Ready and waiting. Drifter, we have to make it quick. If you're not there, we can't wait."

"Understood, Island Station. We'll be there. The girls are packed."

"Drifter," Harald said the name deliberately. "Travel light. Only what you can carry. We'll radio to the handheld when we're close—channel six."

"Copy that," Mark said. There was a catch in his voice. "... Thank you, Island Station..."

Harald kept his voice steady. "Good luck, Drifter. We'll see you tomorrow."

The lugger rocked against the dock, the lines tightening and loosening with the swell. It was just past sunrise, the sky shifting from grey to blue. Peter tied down the life jackets for the Drifter children. Callum hoisted the sails, letting them flap in the light morning air.

Harald, Erik, and a few other early risers stood on the dock. Cari and Lina came down the path together, each carrying a cloth-wrapped bundle. Cari handed one to Peter. "For the crossing," she said.

Lina passed the second to Callum. "This one's for them," she said. "They'll need something real to eat."

"Callum, keep the handheld turned on," Erik said. "We'll monitor six. Let us know you're safe. We should be able to pick up a signal a few miles offshore."

Callum lifted a hand in acknowledgment, then turned and pulled in the mainsheet. No words—his focus was on the boat and the job.

The lugger eased away from the dock with barely a word. The hull creaked softly as it caught the swell, the sail drawing just enough wind to steady her course. Callum stood at the tiller, eyes ahead, while Peter moved quietly between tasks, checking lines, adjusting trim.

Behind them, Talem receded—first the figures on the dock, then the trees along the bluff, then everything but the faint ridge of land against the sky. Ahead, the mainland waited, low and smudged in the morning haze.

They would cross wide, then follow the coast south. Landmarks would come in time.

For now, it was open water and the slow rhythm of the boat beneath their feet.

The lugger held a steady line across the channel. The wind worked with them, speeding the passage. The mainland coast drew into view—no longer just shape and haze, but details. Tree lines. Broken rooftops. Smoke.

Not one column. Several. Rising along the coastline, and further inland. Too many for hearth fires, too far apart for a single fire front. They watched, uneasy.

Callum shifted course, drawing them in tighter than they'd planned. The landmarks were in sight now—the inlet, the ridge above the beach, the mouth of the river.

They had their bearings. What pulled them closer was curiosity.

As they neared the edge of a town, the picture sharpened. Sagging buildings. A collapsed dock. A billboard flapping in the wind, half torn from its frame. Then a figure—sudden—darting across a road, between buildings, arms pumping, head low. Running from something. Or toward it.

Peter stood in the bow. "That's close enough."

Callum was already turning the rudder, angling back out to sea.

Close enough for landmarks. No closer.

Mark glanced back once, taking in the barge for the last time. It had been home, but he wouldn't miss it.

He'd got the girls moving early. None of them had slept well—not even Lisa. They were worried. He was worried. Too many things could go wrong. Too many ways to miss the window. He wasn't going to be the reason they missed it.

They reached the beach without trouble. It was exactly where it should be—just north of the river mouth, marked clean on the map, just as Harald had said. A flat sweep of sand, backed by dunes and scattered driftwood. From the ridge above, he could see all the way down to the water.

But it wasn't empty.

A fire was burning near the edge of the beach. Not huge, but enough to throw smoke. A few figures moved near it. One bent low, another walked the perimeter. Then a shout. Or maybe a scream. Mark couldn't tell. The wind muddled it.

But he was sure of one thing—this wasn't going to work.

They backed off the ridge, crouched in the dune grass. Loretta looked up at him, waiting. He didn't speak. Just motioned for silence.

They'd passed a cove on the way in—tighter, stony, hard to spot from the water. No signs of life. It could work.

It would have to.

They backtracked, moving low along the dune line.

He'd been right. The cove could work. Not perfect— but it was hard to remember a time when anything had been perfect.

They made it down to the water, sheltered beneath an undercut rock. The tide was out. Wet sand under their boots. Mark retrieved the radio.

Channel six.

The handheld crackled in Peter's hand.

"... Island Station, this is Drifter."

Peter brought the radio up. "Copy, Drifter. Go ahead."

"The beach is no good. People there—fire, movement. We've shifted. A cove just south. It's tight, just the other side of the gridline. Do you see it?"

Peter checked the map. "Copy that, Drifter. We've got your position. Sit tight."

He looked at Callum, who had already changed course.

Callum pushed the tiller over, bringing the lugger to the wind, steering them back out to sea. He didn't like it. Neither did Peter. But sailing straight into the cove from here would put them in full view of the beach—and whoever was gathered there.

They looped wide, tracing a long, slow arc toward the mouth of the river. From there, they could come in from the south, with the cove mostly screened by a low headland.

"Not ideal," Peter said quietly, more to himself than to Callum. "But it'll do."

As they approached, Peter scanned the shoreline through a handheld scope. The cove came into view—a stony inlet tucked beneath the bluff. No sign of movement. But the beach wasn't far. If someone walked north along the waterline, they'd see it. No way around that now.

Peter clicked the mic again. "Drifter, we're inbound. Hold position."

A brief reply: "Understood."

He zipped the radio into a pocket and dropped into a crouch beside the gunwale, heart in his throat.

Callum steered straight into the cove. Wind at their back. Loosening the sails just off the shelving shore, the lugger eased up, gently crunching into sand and stone, stopping in knee-deep water.

They didn't speak as the girls climbed aboard—Loretta first, then Lisa, hand in hand. Mark followed, his boots sloshing in the shallows. Peter helped them over the gunwale, keeping movements quiet and steady. No questions. No explanations.

Callum had already turned the bow off the beach. He worked the sail, caught the wind just enough to pull them free. Not enough room for a clean run out—he had to beat upwind, tacking three times to get them clear of the cove.

On the last tack, Peter looked back.

The fire on the beach was still burning. Figures moved near it—four, maybe five. One crouched low. Another stood with something in their hands. Watching. But not toward the cove. Not toward the boat.

They hadn't seen them.

Peter reached beneath the thwart and pulled out the cloth-wrapped bundle. He handed it to Loretta, who opened it slowly—bread, cheese, a handful of dried berries, three apples. She divided it without a word, passing pieces to Lisa and Mark.

Callum didn't turn. He was focused on the water ahead, trimming the sail and checking their angle to the wind. Then he reached into the side pouch and brought out the compass. He studied it a moment, nodded once, and stowed it again.

"Straight to Talem," he said. It was the first thing he'd said since the pickup.

No one answered, but they all understood.

They were done with the mainland.

The lugger held its line, the coast falling behind them in haze and silence. No need to linger. No reason to look back.

The girls slept as they made the crossing, curled beside each other in the bow. Mark kept watch, eyes never far from the horizon. Peter stayed near them, easing the sheet lines when the gusts picked up. Callum held course, radioing in as they got close.

By late afternoon, the shoreline of Talem came into view—first the dark shape of the headland, then the low curve of the harbor, then the dock itself, lined with waiting figures.

The lugger eased in, Callum feathering the sail before they reached the mooring. Ropes were caught. Hands reached out. Lisa was carried ashore in someone's arms. Loretta followed, blinking in the low light.

Mark was about to step onto the dock when a hand reached down. A firm grip helped him up out of the boat.

"I'm Harald," the boy said. "I've been waiting for this."

They made their way up to the town meeting hall. Tables had been laid—white cloths and cutlery. A place for everyone. The space was alive with the low buzz of conversation. Eyes moved to Mark, then to Loretta, and finally to Lisa. Glances caught, smiles lingerin g.

The meal was simple in the Talem tradition. Fresh bread, baked squash, a stew carried in from the hearth. As people relaxed and a few began to move, someone called out across the room.

"What about a story, Grace?"

Grace was seated in the middle of the room. She didn't move. People drew toward her. Mark turned his chair in her direction.

"There was a village once," she began. Lisa's eyes widened and Loretta reached for her hand.

"Built at the bend of a river. The people were known for their generosity—but they were also careful. In every home, two baskets hung by the door.

"One was for the family. The other was for neighbors. Food went in when there was extra. It was a quiet system, and it worked.

"But in the square at the center of town, there hung a third basket. It wasn't tied to any one home. It was for strangers—those just passing through, or those with nowhere else to go.

"In good years, all three baskets were filled. The third basket never overflowed, but there was always something: dried beans, a crust of bread, sometimes a blanket or a bundle of herbs.

"Then came a season of drought. The river ran low. Gardens failed. One by one, the baskets emptied—first the one in the square, then the ones for neighbors. People still filled their own, but did it quietly, eyes down.

"One morning, three children appeared at the edge of the village. No parents. No words. Just tired feet and hollow eyes. The villagers gathered. They argued. They did the math.

"That night, no decision was made.

"But at first light, the third basket was full. No one said who had done it. But the next night, it was full again. And again after that.

"When the rains finally came and the river returned, the village took stock of what it had lost. And found it hadn't lost anything at all."

CHAPTER NINETEEN

MARK WOKE EARLY. The girls were still sleeping as he stepped out into the cool of the morning.

They'd spent the night in a house set aside for guests—though it was clear there hadn't been any in a long time. The beds were clean and comfortable. The blankets faded, but warm. Someone had left a small tin of homemade biscuits on the table.

He stood for a moment on the porch, unsure where to start. The path curved down toward town, so he followed it.

The way bowed gently, then opened up to buildings he'd seen the night before. The dock stretched out into the small natural harbor. Beyond it, the supply warehouses—low structures, square and neat.

He raised his eyes.

Behind the town stood the caldera. He hadn't missed it yesterday, but in the morning light it seemed to tower over everything. Covered with green—trees, bushes, grasses—it looked alive and ancient at once. Mark had a feeling it had been something else before—and might be again.

He paused to take it in, understanding—almost unconsciously—how this mountain defined the island.

The town itself was compact. Buildings close together, but not crowded. Paths well-worn. A bicycle leaned against a rail. A line of laundry hung between two porches, sleeves swaying gently in the breeze.

Many of the houses were occupied. A few were boarded—waiting for better days.

He wandered past the meeting hall and paused outside the open door. The tables were still there, white cloths now gathered in loose piles, dishes washed and drying. Someone swept the floor in slow arcs.

He remembered sitting there the night before—the food, the firelight, Grace's story.

For a moment, it felt like it had all happened somewhere else—to someone else. Not because it was a dream, but because it didn't belong to the same world he'd come from.

His gaze moved again to the caldera. Tracing its outline, his vision moved from top to bottom this time. At the base he saw it—a trail, faint but visible. He followed its path as it snaked up the mountain.

He moved, slowly at first, then with more purpose, until he was climbing. Ascending steadily. Breathing in the forest—pine and juniper, dry needles underfoot, the occasional scatter of loose stone. The trees thinned as he rose, revealing more of the sky. Wind pushed through the branches, carrying a faint resinous scent.

He didn't pass anyone. No voices, no distant sounds. Just the crunch of his boots and the steady pull of his breath.

Halfway up, the trail turned into switchbacks. The footing narrowed. He kept going.

At the top, the path leveled briefly, then spilled out onto open rock. The view stopped him cold.

The island stretched in all directions—old growth rising like green towers to the north, the clustered rooftops of the village below, the water folding outward like a sheet of hammered light. Off to the northeast, Nameth sat still and grey behind the haze, squared-off and orderly.

And beyond that, barely visible in the smudged distance—the mainland.

Rising from the haze he saw the smoke. Columns, rising then drifting, becoming lost as they merged with the sky. Faint flickers of orange showed in places, the fire feeding on what no longer was.

He felt it in his legs first, his knees gave a little. He sat down hard on the stone.

He had managed. Through the river, through the cold nights, the gnawing fear—but now it spilled through. The loss. His parents. Gone. A world that was never coming back.

He didn't hold it. It came and he sat—his hands gripping his knees tight to his chest.

Time passed. He wasn't sure how much. But finally he rose. He took in the island one more time. His vision didn't stray east. He turned, starting a slow descent to something new.

By the time Mark reached the edge of town the sun was higher. Shadows shortened, and the bright light of day had the people of Talem moving with quiet purpose.

He was back at the Town Hall when he saw Harald, crouched with a screwdriver, adjusting the brakes on a child's bike. Harald gave the lever a final squeeze, satisfied, then looked up.

Mark slowed but didn't speak.

"You made it," Harald said, rising and brushing his hands on his pants. "We've all been pulling for you. It's good that you're here."

Mark nodded. His mouth felt dry. He wasn't ready to talk.

Harald reached around and placed the screwdriver in the back pocket of his work pants. "Come on," he said. "I'll give you the tour," he grinned at Mark. "Should take about five minutes."

Mark managed half a smile and followed.

They walked side by side. Harald pointed out the study hall and the library.

"I didn't used to go there much," he said. "But it's actually quite good. You don't need a membership," he quipped.

They walked down to Supply and then back up to the workshop, Harald finally steering Mark over to the hydro setup.

"This is new," Harald said, face lighting up. "We can run machines in the shop, charge all our batteries. We're even working on a second unit."

"Most of this runs on what we can fix," he added. "Or repurpose. My dad and Callum worked to bring things in from all over. You'd be amazed at what's in there."

They crossed a footbridge and came up on a wide clearing where a few kids were setting up buckets near a row of rain barrels. One of them waved. Harald waved back.

"No one's really in charge," he said. "But everyone kind of knows what needs doing."

Mark said nothing, but the rhythm of walking helped. The motion steadied him. The world felt a little more upright.

They stopped near a flat boulder where someone had carved a sundial long ago. Harald glanced at it, then at the sky.

Mark looked out across the clearing.

"Harald... what happened to all your people?"

Harald looked away before answering.

"People started leaving the island about fifteen years ago. There were shortages. That's when my mom and dad came—kind of going the opposite direction from everyone else."

He paused, then met Mark's eyes.

"I wasn't born here. But Lina was. My mom died giving birth. Complications. There weren't any doctors then. They'd all left too."

Mark held Harald's gaze. Then the two boys kept walking, Harald pointing out another feature of Talem as they moved into the light.

They circled back toward the harbor. Light angled in over the roofs, catching the radio tower that rose just behind the station building—thin and unassuming, but unmistakably deliberate.

Harald led them up the steps and heaved on the door which always resisted being opened.

Inside, the room was cool and orderly. A narrow desk stretched along a wall, lined with notebooks, an old clock, and a series of mismatched radios. Wires ran like veins across the wall, feeding into solar-charged battery banks below.

Sarah looked up from the logbook. "Thought I heard someone," she said. "Come to check the heartbeat?"

Harald gestured toward Mark. "Figured he might like to see how it works."

Sarah smiled and rose from the chair. "Well, it's not much to look at. But it's how we listen. And how we let people know we're still here."

She showed him the frequencies they monitored, the call logs, how they rotated shifts—morning, midday, evening. Mark followed her explanations closely, asking a few quiet questions about range and signal bounce.

Sarah pointed to the UHF set up that let them communicate with the outlying farms, "This one's been active this morning. Words out that we have some new residents on the island."

Harald raised an eyebrow. The drums were beating.

"You had a shortwave setup on the barge." she continued.

Mark nodded. "We had a kit rigged up on the barge. My dad taught me the basics. We mostly listened. Didn't transmit unless we had to."

Sarah's expression softened. "Smart. That kind of caution probably kept you safe."

She paused, then tilted her head. "If you ever want to sit in—cover a shift or two—I'd be glad to have you. It's not just radios. It's connection."

Mark looked around the room again. The gear was worn, but cared for. There was a chair open beside hers.

"Yeah," he said. "Maybe I will."

Sarah nodded, then reached to adjust the dial, the static rising again like wind in the trees.

Lina led Loretta and Lisa up the worn steps of the library, her hand resting lightly on the railing.

"They've got everything in here," she said. "Novels, field guides, old encyclopedias. Some of it's even funny."

Lisa didn't respond. She was trailing a few paces behind, her face unreadable. Loretta, on the other hand, nodded earnestly. "We read a lot on the barge," she said. "Mostly old schoolbooks. My dad kept a set of classics in a crate."

Lina smiled and pushed open the door. "Then you'll like this."

Inside, the room was warm and still. Rows of mismatched shelves held books sorted by hand, some labeled, others not. Behind a low desk, reading glasses perched halfway down her nose, sat Grace.

"Good morning," she said without looking up. "You must be the three L's. Welcome to our world of learning."

Loretta gave a small, polite laugh. Lisa glanced at the shelves.

Grace looked up, taking in all three of them, eyes resting on each girl just long enough to see beneath the surface.

"I'll be quiet," she said, setting her notebook aside. "But I'm here if you need anything."

Lina gestured toward a corner. "That shelf over there has the illustrated stuff. Field guides, atlases, old museum books."

Lisa moved first, surprising them. She drifted toward the shelf and crouched low, running her fingers along the spines.

Loretta followed more slowly, pausing to read the titles aloud under her breath, as if proving she still belonged to the world of learning.

Lina wandered off for a moment, giving them space.

Grace remained at her desk, head tilted slightly, watching with a calm that didn't intrude.

Lisa stopped at a thin book with a blue cloth cover. She pulled it down slowly—a bird guide, the kind with beautifully hand-drawn illustrations. Almost a work of art. Her thumb traced a page with a cedar waxwing. Her mouth opened as she took in the fine drawings. Then, glancing over her shoulder, she slipped it into the front pocket of her coat.

Grace saw.

But she didn't speak.

Instead, she stood and walked to the far window, pretending to inspect the latch.

Loretta, nearby, had seen nothing. She was holding a thick book about volcanoes and explaining something to no one in particular about lava tubes. Her voice was even, cheerful, too bright.

Lina returned and offered a light smile. "Find anything good?"

Loretta held up her book like a badge. "This one."

Grace turned from the window. "You're welcome to take what you like. Just let Lina or me know, so we can mark it down. We try not to lose track of things, that's all."

Lisa looked at the floor. Loretta nodded quickly for both of them.

"Of course," she said.

Grace smiled, kind but clear.

The children spent the next half hour exploring the shelves, exclaiming when they discovered an unusual book. Loretta had pulled out *What to Expect When You're Expecting,* Lina giggled too.

They were headed to the door when Grace stood and pointed toward the corner. "We've got bean bags," she said. "They're a rare and ancient technology. Why don't you stay a minute."

Grace walked to a nearby shelf and ran her fingers along the spines. She paused, pulled down a worn green volume, and turned it in her hands.

"This one's stayed with us," she said. "Not fancy, but it knows a few things."

She returned to the corner and sat on the edge of a low bench. The girls settled deeper into the beanbags as Grace opened the book.

The Wind in the Willows. By Kenneth Grahame.

She didn't announce it—just began. Her voice low and even, letting the language do the work. Mole's restlessness. Rat's boat. The river, constant and quiet. The way the world could feel lost and found at the same time.

As she read, the room retreated. The edges of the day blurred. Loretta leaned in, her expression softening. Lisa's eyes stayed on the page, though her posture didn't change. But her shoulders dropped, just slightly.

When Grace reached the end of a chapter, she closed the book gently.

There was a hush in the room.

Loretta stood first. "Thank you," she whispered.

Lisa didn't speak. She moved toward the door, hands in her coat pockets.

Grace watched them go.

At the shelf near the window, Lisa paused. With a small glance over her shoulder, she slipped the bird guide from her coat and slid it between two books on the lower shelf. It landed softly, right where it belonged.

Grace didn't move. Just gave the smallest nod.

That evening found the Drifters near the steps of the Town Hall. Lisa and Jake tossed a rubber ball back and forth while Loretta and Mark sat, faces turned to the warmth of the low sun.

Erik came up from the west road, boots dusty and jacket unzipped. He gave a quick nod to Mark and crouched, retying a loose lace. "I was down at the Harrison farm earlier," he said, more to the space between them than to anyone in particular.

"They heard," he added, "about your arrival. Reid and Marla."

Mark looked up, cautious.

"They'd like to have you for a little while," Erik said. "No pressure. Just a change of pace. An invitation." Loretta was watching now. "They enjoyed having Harald and Lina during the harvest. Said it felt good to share the land a bit."

He glanced at Lisa, then at Loretta. "It's quiet down there. Goats, apples, morning mist. They thought it might be good for you all. A slower start. Just until you feel more settled."

"They could use a little help," Erik went on. "We volunteered Peter, but the three of you could make a difference... for a little while."

Loretta looked to Mark, uncertain.

Lisa stared at the sky.

Mark nodded slowly. "Okay," he said. "We'd like that."

Erik rose and gave a small smile. "They'll be glad."

Harald and Lina had wandered up, and Lina grabbed Loretta's hand. "They have the best sleeping loft, and Marla is an amazing cook. We'll come visit."

Harald nudged Mark, "I hope you know how to fix things. Reid's always breaking something or other."

CHAPTER TWENTY

BREE WOKE to the sound of shoes on concrete. Feet pacing the walkway outside the bunkhouse. Headed to work in the fields, or on the vertical beds. She must have overslept. She was assigned to the greenhouses this week. Picking fruit. Emptying pots. Filling pots.

She pulled on her sweater and stepped into line for wash up. At least there was hot water. But no one spoke much in the mornings anymore. Conversation meant questions, and questions had started to feel risky.

She spotted her father in the dining hall. Seated with Clare. She thought about joining them but their heads were together. She didn't want to interrupt. She sat with Sammy. She was safe. Kept her head down and did the work. No complaining or arguments.

The day unfolded as expected. She worked on the tomato vines, thinned greens. What she wouldn't give for some music. She'd had headphones once.

She headed for lunch around midday. The greenhouse was stifling hot. She wasn't sure if she had the resolve for the afternoon shift. But you worked your assignment. That was a given.

By late afternoon Bree was exhausted. The heat from the greenhouse. The mind numbing work tending the plants. She headed back to the bunkhouse to lie down. To cool down.

She passed the comms room. There was a notice posted: ALL RADIO TRAFFIC MUST BE CLEARED THROUGH CENTRAL. That was new.

She passed it without pausing.

That evening, she slipped into comms. Technically off-limits after dark, but no one patrolled closely anymore.

The UHF was warm to the touch. She turned the dial gently, listening for the background pulse of the Talem band.

"Island contact. This is Nameth Unit Six."

Bree and Lina had agreed to reach out in the evenings. Sometimes they connected. Sometimes they didn't. Tonight would be a good night to hear her voice.

Static. Then a click.

"Go ahead, Unicorn Six."

Bree smiled faintly at the old call sign. She kept her voice low.

"Just wanted to say hey. Things are... fine. You know. Still vertical."

She hesitated. "I was thinking about you and those apples you brought last time. I can still remember the taste. That's all. Just wanted to say that."

Lina didn't fill the silence too quickly. "It's good to hear your voice."

Bree exhaled, slow. "Yours too."

She waited another moment. Then clicked off the mic, turned down the gain, and slipped out into the night.

CHAPTER TWENTY-ONE

LINA, CARI, AND HARALD sat at the dock, legs swinging from the seawall on the oceanside. They were killing time—on break from the workshop. The copied hydro unit was nearly finished. It wasn't pretty, but it would work. The island had built something real. Something useful. They'd pushed the limits of their tools and knowledge, but soon it would be ready to install. Two hydros wouldn't power a new world—but they'd add a little capacity, and more importantly, resilience. Insurance against failure. A second thread in the weave.

They chatted easily, letting the conversation drift— workshop repairs, something Grace had said in the library, then finally, the Drifters.

"We should head down there," Lina said. "Maybe even see if we could stay the night. Six people in that sleeping loft would be fun."

Harald rolled his eyes. "Not sure Reid and Marla would call that fun. But yeah, we should visit. We can take the bikes." He glanced at Cari. "I'll race you."

Cari leaned back on her elbows. "I've got a better idea. What about the old Sunfish in the boatyard? No one uses it. We could sail down, leave it in the Wren boathouse. Might come in handy down there."

Lina shifted. "How do you think they're doing? The Drifters."

Harald paused. "Tough road. I don't think they're okay. Not really. But staying with Reid and Marla's probably as close as you get to being wrapped in cotton wool."

"Yeah," Lina agreed. "If your wool blanket hauls you out to the orchard at first light and hands you a picking basket."

Cari laughed. "Was it really that bad?"

Harald grinned. "Not at all. But I've got a feeling Lina's going to develop a sudden medical condition next apple season. Something that requires treatment at the clinic."

They fell silent for a while.

Lina glanced toward the clinic. She wondered if Jana needed help with anything. She liked it there—something about the quiet rhythm, the way the cabinets were labeled in neat handwriting. Hamish could be a little dry, but Jana made up for it.

Cari stole a glance at Harald. She wasn't sure what she was looking for—maybe signs of tension, maybe just weather in his eyes. Were there any storms on the horizon? She'd noticed they did well together in storms.

Harald looked out to sea. The small harbor curled around the southwest corner of the island. The deep blue of the open water settled him. He traced the horizon with his eyes and wondered—how far was it to Japan? Could they make it in the lugger?

Then, just at the edge of his vision, something caught.

A shape—subtle, out on the line he'd been staring at. A break in the clean edge of sea and sky.

He touched Cari's hand. "Do you see that?"

He pointed, and the two girls followed his gaze, squinting against the bright water, eyes narrowing as they searched the distant swell.

They watched.

For a few minutes, nothing happened. The shape was definitely moving, slowly—just enough to catch a glint. Not a wave, then. Not driftwood.

"A sail," Cari murmured.

It tilted in the wind, a pale triangle folding against the haze. The boat beneath it came into view gradually, hull low and narrow, angled slightly toward the island.

They stayed where they were, legs still dangling, eyes tracking its progress. It wasn't fast. Just steady. Like someone knew where they were going and didn't mind how long it took to get there.

Lina squinted. "It's changing course."

The boat had angled more sharply now, unmistakably heading toward Talem's southern shore.

Lina rose, brushing her hands on her pants. "I'm going to get Dad," she said, casually. Like she was announcing she needed more firewood. "Just in case."

She didn't run. Just walked off with a slow, familiar stride, leaving Cari and Harald on the seawall, watching the lone sail draw nearer.

By the time the sailboat approached the harbor a crowd had gathered. Erik and Grace. Even Callum was there.

The boat dropped its main and, instead of heading for the dock, pirouetted into the wind with practiced ease. There was a splash, and the sound of chain letting out.

The boat stern shifted with the slight swell. At anchor. Someone stepped forward on deck—hard to see clearly, backlit by the sun. Then another shape emerged beside them. A second person. Both moved with practiced ease.

Voices murmured on shore but no one called out. It wasn't fear exactly. Just the weight of uncertainty, everyone waiting to see how this would unfold.

The figures on the boat didn't wave. They didn't shout. One of them leaned against the rail, scanning the dock, the hillside, the watching faces.

Then—finally—a voice called out, low but clear.

"We're headed north," it said. "We saw your harbor and thought we might visit. Would that be alright?"

Erik stepped forward a pace. "It can be. Depends what you're looking for."

The figure nodded once, unthreatened. "Rest, mostly. Water. Maybe a conversation or two."

A pause.

Then Erik raised a hand, just a small gesture.

"Alright," he said. "Let's talk. We'll come to you."

Harald steadied the oars while Erik coiled the painter at the bow. The boat bumped gently against the dock as they pushed off. Behind them, voices had grown quieter, the murmuring crowd content to let the island speak through the two of them.

The strangers waited at the rail, hands visible, postures relaxed. No weapons. Just sun-weathered clothes and steady eyes.

"Let's keep it warm," Erik murmured. "Neutral. You're not just rowing, you're reading."

Harald nodded. He was already watching—how they stood, how they glanced at one another, whether their hands betrayed nerves or ease.

The small boat bumped gently against the sailboat's hull. Harald tied off the painter to the rear ladder.

"Permission to come aboard?" Erik said, slipping into protocol.

"Of course, of course," the two men replied almost in unison. "Come up and join us in the cockpit."

Harald climbed the ladder behind his father, scanning the deck as he rose. The sailboat wasn't big, about thirty-five feet, maybe a little more. Through the open companionway, he caught a glimpse of the cabin below—a compact galley, a narrow berth forward. Cramped, but seaworthy. You could cross oceans in a boat like that. People had.

The boat—and its crew—were shipshape. A place for everything, and everything in its place. The lines on deck were coiled and lashed with care. Below, Harald could see the same: nothing loose, everything stowed, as if for weather. As if they were always ready to move.

The men didn't offer handshakes.

"I'm Victor. This is Julian."

Victor was the one speaking, Harald noted. But he wasn't sure what that meant—yet. He'd have to pay attention.

An awkward silence followed. Erik didn't move to fill it, and Harald had already decided his role here was to listen.

Eventually Victor spoke again. "We've been sailing up the coast... for a while." He didn't look at Julian.

"We could do to fill our water tanks, if that's possible. Maybe trade for a little food. Fruit or vegetables. We can offer labor—we don't have much else."

"Where are you coming from?" Erik asked. "Looks like you've been on the water a while."

He must've noticed the hull too. As Harald had climbed aboard, he'd seen it clearly—barnacles and algae thick below the waterline. A slow accumulation. They hadn't hauled out in months.

Harald also noted what Erik hadn't done: he hadn't addressed the man's request. He was still probing.

"We're really not coming from anywhere at this point," Victor said. Julian nodded along, but it was Victor who kept speaking. "The coast isn't safe. We've been picking our way north. Mostly anchoring in bays—we'll go ashore if things are right. But there's a lot of places where things aren't right."

"Thought we might head north. Way north." Victor's voice trailed off, like the words had run out—or he didn't trust the next ones. "Less people, less trouble."

"I'm a chef," Julian said at last. He glanced at Victor, who gave a small nod—almost imperceptible.

"If we're welcome ashore, I'd be glad to cook something. It's been a long time since we ate somewhere that wasn't rocking."

"We'll talk it over," Erik said, rising. "I'll send word later today. I'm sure we can work something out. Welcome to Talem."

His words were polite, but not warm—and Harald caught the gap. The tone didn't quite match the message. He had the sense they weren't getting the whole story. And Erik, he was certain of it.

The path rose gently from the harbor. They walked in silence at first, boots crunching on the worn trail, wind tugging at their jackets. The sailboat bobbed behind them.

Harald glanced at his father but said nothing.

Eventually Erik spoke. "They're well ordered. Did you notice?"

"Yeah," Harald said. "Deck was clean. Below too. Everything stowed like they're still on passage."

Erik nodded. "People don't stay that disciplined unless they're under orders. Or giving them."

Harald waited. He knew the look in Erik's eye—he was still thinking it through, undecided.

"They've seen some things," Erik went on. "Victor's calm, but that kind of calm takes effort. Julian's not calm. He's watching Victor."

"Julian only spoke when Victor let him," Harald said.

"That too."

They walked a few more paces. At a bend in the trail, the town came into view—rooftops tucked among the trees, smoke curling from a few chimneys.

"You think it's true? About the coast?"

Erik took a while to answer. "Probably. Doesn't mean they told us all of it."

Harald stopped. "Are you going to let them come ashore?"

Erik looked at him. "We already did."

He let the words settle, then added, "They can come to the house. We'll get Grace. Callum too. You come. Bring your eyes. And your ears."

The aroma of herbs and spices simmering on the range had Harald's attention before dinner was even served. Lina kept wandering through the kitchen, craning her neck to see what was being added to the pot.

"We're going to need the recipe, Julian," she said. "This smells too good to only eat once."

Grace sat at the table, watching with a half-smile, elbows resting. Callum, his back to the wall, sipped cider slowly. He drank like a person who knew to savor things.

Victor was already seated, stiff in his chair. Harald thought he looked like someone waiting for a bill he didn't want to pay.

"It's been a while since someone cooked like this," Grace said. "And even longer since they cleaned up as they went."

Julian had used half a dozen pans, but each one was washed and hung back in its place.

Julian gave a quick smile but didn't speak. Victor answered instead. "We're used to earning our keep."

Harald sat near the stove, on a stool just out of Julian's way. He watched both men. Victor—alert, unreadable. Julian had relaxed as he cooked, but still checked in with Victor from time to time, as if asking permission.

The meal itself was simple—a thick fish stew, potatoes, greens from the island garden. All familiar ingredients, but arranged in a way that felt... refined. Julian finally joined them at the table but didn't serve himself until everyone else had started eating.

The first few bites passed in silence, each person taking a moment to enjoy the warmth, the flavor.

Then Grace set down her fork. "You said you've been coming up the coast."

Victor nodded. "From the south. Way down there."

"Mainland?" she asked.

He hesitated. "No. Offshore."

He and Julian exchanged a glance. Victor let out a slow breath, like he'd been holding it far too long.

"We were on a boat," Julian said, picking up the thread. "A big one. Superyacht. Full crew, owners, their kids."

"We had fuel," Victor added. "Not enough to go anywhere far. The captain was rationing. Marinas were stripped. No one wanted to be tied up and visible."

Grace's smile had faded. She said nothing.

"We were anchored," Julian said more quietly. "Someone must have seen the lights."

"What happened?" Erik asked. His voice was nearly a whisper.

The men paused. Finally Victor said, "They came at night. Three boats. Boarded us. Took everything."

"They killed the captain first," Julian said. His voice caught. "Then the family. Machetes and knives."

"It's a bad time to be rich," Victor said. "They took the female crew. Let the rest of us go. Hired hands—we weren't the problem."

Harald didn't know what to feel—pity, anger, relief that it hadn't been them.

Callum leaned forward. "And the sailboat?"

"We took the tender," Victor said. "Worked our way up the coast. Found the sailboat on a mooring. No sign of the owner. We waited a day. Then left."

There was no judgment in Callum's face. Just the question: "How far have you sailed?"

"Three, four thousand miles," Julian said. "Carefully."

"I wanted to head west," Victor said. "To the islands. But no satnav. No charts. I'm a first mate, not Thor Heyerdahl. So we went north instead."

He paused. "We're not out of ideas. Just running low on options."

Julian worked the next day, helping Tommy reorganize shelving in Supply. The following day, Grace had him work with the kids in Study Hall, teaching them a little of his trade. Victor stayed on the sailboat. He filled the tanks, and townspeople brought what fresh produce they could spare.

On the third morning, the sailboat was gone. Slipped out just after dawn. No goodbyes.

Harald stood on the bluff above the harbor and watched their sails angle north—north, but away from land. They had what they needed. No need to come ashore again. He wasn't sure they'd find what they were looking for, but they knew how to leave a place without taking more than they'd earned.

CHAPTER TWENTY-TWO

THE SUNFISH MOVED LAZILY toward the harbor entrance, its hull low in the water under the weight of three crew and a packed duffel. The small cockpit felt even tighter with all of them aboard, each shift in weight drawing a subtle response from the boat. They worked to keep the overloaded craft steady in the light wind. The breeze would pick up and hold it stable once they cleared the headland and reached open water, heading north toward Wren.

Cari sat at the helm, relaxed but alert, while Lina trimmed the main. Harald let them take the lead. He didn't mind—he liked watching them work the boat, the quiet coordination of it. His thoughts drifted ahead to the Harrisons' farm, to seeing Mark and his sisters again. It felt good, this kind of trip.

The land on the starboard side seemed impossibly green. Second-growth trees crowded the shoreline, thick with new tips, pushing toward the light. Alder and spruce tangled together along the bank, and the scent of salt and resin hung in the air.

Harald had been surprised when Erik suggested they stay the night. Something about a fence that needed mending—but Harald suspected that was just an excuse. Either way, the extra time would be welcome. The girls were already excited for the sleepover. He wondered if Mark might find some peace—if that was even possible. And the younger girls—Marla would keep them busy with chores and food, keep their hands moving and their minds anchored. They were in a better place now than they'd been on the river. He just hoped Talem would never be tested like that.

As predicted, the wind freshened as they headed north—an easy sail. Harald moved to the foredeck, weight balanced at center. He trailed a hand in the water, droplets of spray cool against his face. They passed a kelp bed stretching in long golden skeins near the shallows. A cormorant dove, vanishing with barely a ripple.

Then, off their port side, a sleek black fluke broke the surface—silent, immense, and gone in a breath. Orca. Harald straightened, eyes scanning the water, but it didn't resurface. Just that one glimpse. Cari saw it too—she gave a low whistle and grinned.

Before they knew it, Wren Cove came into view. Cari angled the Sunfish toward the boathouse, where they planned to store it. Erik hadn't objected when they said they'd sail down—but Harald had seen the raised eyebrow. He wasn't sure his father understood why they'd leave the boat there. Still, if they wanted to slog the near ten miles home on foot tomorrow, that was their business.

The boathouse was empty, but the old manual lift still worked. With a bit of muscle, they cranked the Sunfish out of the water and onto the rails. They stowed the sail, rudder, and tiller on a shelf by the wall, careful to keep everything dry.

Harald glanced around. If they ever needed a quick trip to Nameth, this would be the way—someone could bike down, launch the Sunfish, and be across in no time. But with things the way they were, a trip to Nameth didn't seem likely anytime soon.

They stepped out into the warmth of the day, the door thudding closed behind them. A gravel path led toward the old mansion, thick with weeds and flanked by tangled blackberry and a sagging split-rail fence.

"Think Marla's got something baking?" Lina asked, already halfway up the slope. "Feels like we deserve a pie."

"She's probably got us picking beans before we even get a hello," Cari said, handing the duffel to Harald. "Bet she's been saving chores just for this moment."

They climbed through the lower Wren grounds to the west road, sunlight flickering through alder leaves above them. It was only a few hundred yards to the Harrison farm—the last home out this way. When the old homestead crested into view, Harald slowed a little. The place looked tidier than he remembered. Someone had cleared the path to the shed. A fresh line of laundry shifted on the breeze. On the porch, he spotted Loretta, broom in hand, sweeping wide arcs, while Lisa scrubbed the outdoor table.

"Looks like we're too late to pick up any chores," Harald said. "This place is looking sharp."

Loretta looked up. "Harald!" she shouted, setting aside the broom and running to meet them.

Lina and Cari caught her in a tight hug. Harald glanced past them—Lisa stood by the table, smiling. He gave a small wave, and she crossed the porch to join the embrace.

The screen door creaked open, and Marla stepped outside, drying her hands on her kitchen apron.

"Well," she said, smiling. "We were just about to take a break. Reid and Mark should be down anytime."

"What are they up to?" Harald asked.

"A better question might be what they're *not* up to," Marla replied with a grimace. "Mostly figuring out ways to create more work around here." She glanced toward Loretta and Lisa. "Luckily, we found some good help from the mainland."

They were drinking tea when Reid and Mark appeared from behind the house. Mark's face was already beginning to tan in that particular way that came from long days outside. The color almost matched Reid's, though it lacked the deep-set lines etched by years of farming.

"Finally, you've come back for a shift," Reid said, eyeing Harald and Lina. "And brought a helper," he added, nodding at Cari. "Although, to be honest, I think

Mark and I have things humming along pretty sweetly these days."

Harald glanced at the ground, half wondering what Reid was planning for them, and half wondering how Mark had managed to win over the old curmudgeon so easily.

Marla broke the moment. "You're all off the clock for the afternoon," she said. "Though I *do* need you to take a bag and pick some blackberries—for a special treat tonight."

"I spotted a patch near the Wren place on our way up from the boathouse," Cari said. "Maybe we can show the Drifters around over there."

"Yeah," Lina added. "We sailed in today. We've got a boat stashed down there now."

With the afternoon stretched out before them, they headed up the road toward the old Wren mansion. The dust was dry and warm underfoot, sunlight slanting through the trees. It was Mark who suggested they slip off the road and into the woods. The girls took the narrow path ahead, voices rising and falling as they walked. Harald and Mark followed at a quieter pace, talking over Reid's latest ideas.

"He's got a new lease on life, by the looks of things," Harald said.

"Maybe we're good for each other." Mark's mouth curved into the hint of a smile. "He's fun to work with. I think he was running out of steam—with just the two of them."

"Do you think you might stay for a while?" Harald asked.

Mark considered the question. "I think it's best for the girls right now. Lisa's finally starting to open up. It hasn't been easy—you know that."

Harald slowed his pace, thinking about Mark's steadiness, his quiet acceptance of it all. "We should get you some bikes up here," he said. "It's not so far to town from here if you cycle. The Harrisons are great, and I know you fit in here. But... we should see you in town sometimes."

Mark nodded slowly. "Yeah. I know you're right. We just might need a little more time."

Lisa had wandered ahead, quiet as ever, slipping between trunks and ferns while the others lingered as they chatted. They heard the drum of her feet before they saw her—running now, fast and light over the forest floor. She burst back into view, breathless and wide-eyed.

"Come on," she said. "You have to see this. It's amazing."

They followed without question, ducking under low branches and pushing through salal. Lisa led them along a faint trail that dipped, then rose again into a clearing ringed with sword ferns and mossy stumps.

At the center stood a redwood.

It rose far above the surrounding trees—straight and immense, the bark dark and deeply furrowed. Sunlight filtered down through high branches, casting a broken lattice of gold and green across the clearing. At its base, the trunk flared outward into broad, buttressed roots, anchoring it with quiet permanence.

"Whoa," Lina said softly.

Cari circled slowly, craning her neck to see the top. "How old is this?"

"Must be over a hundred years," Harald said, stepping closer. "More, maybe. Someone planted it. Probably when the Wren house was new."

Lisa just stood near the base, one hand resting on the bark. She didn't say anything else, but the way she looked up—it was like she'd found something worth holding on to.

As the afternoon unfolded, Harald showed them the dilapidated mansion—but they didn't go in. He'd been curious about it when he explored alone, but today it didn't fit the mood. Not ominous, exactly. Just... off. Without speaking, they all seemed to agree to keep moving.

They passed the outbuildings on their way back. Harald felt a flicker of something—like a thread left untied—but he let it go.

They picked their blackberries from the brambles near the cove, fingers and tongues stained dark with the juice of the sour fruit. By the time they were finished, the sun was slanting lower across the trees.

Lisa led the way up the path toward the farmhouse. They chatted as they walked, wondering about Marla's special treat. Somehow, when it came to food, Marla never disappointed.

The kitchen was already warm when they stepped inside, the oven ticking softly and the scent of something savory for dinner drifting through the air.

Lisa presented Marla with the bag of blackberries. "We almost filled it," she said.

Marla looked at her hands, then at the others'—all stained deep from the fruit. "Alright," she said, "time to wash up. You can all help with this."

On the long table, Marla had laid out bowls and ingredients: a tin of coarse flour, a crock of soft goat butter, a small jar of honey the color of amber.

"We'll skip the pie crust today," she said, tying her apron tighter. "Too fiddly. Crumble's faster—and just as good, if you ask me."

Lina and Lisa started rinsing the blackberries in a steel bowl at the sink while Loretta peeled apples with practiced turns of the blade. Cari was measuring flour by eye, mixing it with oats and chunks of cold butter in a wide ceramic bowl.

"No sugar?" Harald asked, reaching for a spoon.

Marla gave him a look. "Not unless you've got a bag tucked in your coat. We use honey now. The Conways usually have a little extra. Good stuff—strong flavor, but it works."

Reid, wiping his hands on a towel, added, "I tried tapping the old maples out past the ridge last spring. Didn't get much, but it was sweet." He shrugged and glanced at Mark. "Hard to boil it down without a proper setup. Might try again this year."

"So what you're saying," Cari said, "is this dessert comes with a story."

"Makes you wonder why we ever thought buying a pie was a good idea," Marla replied.

Harald watched as the filling came together—apples and berries tossed with a little flour and a generous spoonful of honey, the topping crumbled over by hand. There were no measuring cups. No timers. Just memory and feel.

After a simple dinner, Marla pulled the crumble from the oven, releasing a rich wave of warm fruit and browned butter. A rich aroma filled the kitchen—sweet, earthy, and unmistakably real.

Lisa leaned in close, eyes half-closed. "It smells like... something I remember. But I don't know from where."

Marla smiled, her voice quiet. "Yes. Wonderful, isn't it?"

Finally, the six kids headed up the ladder to the sleeping loft. It turned out Marla and Reid didn't mind at all if they crammed together. They'd promised no talking—Lina had her fingers firmly crossed, believing that talking *quietly* didn't count anyway.

At the edge of the bedding, Lina paused and looked at Harald, then at Cari.

"Should I sleep between you two?" she asked, not quite teasing.

Cari raised an eyebrow. "Only if you want elbows in your back all night."

Lina smirked and flopped down on the far side, pulling the blanket over her head. "Fine. But I'll know if anything creepy happens."

They laughed, and the moment softened. Cari settled next to Harald and, without saying anything, curled into him, her head resting lightly on his shoulder.

The Drifters were side by side—the way they slept every night. Close enough to lay a hand if someone cried out in the dark.

Outside, wind moved through the trees. The house gave its familiar night sounds—boards creaking, branches brushing the roof. The warmth of the others pressed in from every side.

Harald lay still, staring up at the slanted ceiling. He didn't know what would come next. The world was still uncertain, fragile in its shape.

But this—this was real. This was enough. Warmth, laughter, hands berry-stained, and Cari breathing softly beside him. A full heart, even in a broken world.

He let out a long breath and closed his eyes.

CHAPTER TWENTY-THREE

BREE'S STOMACH HAD BEEN CRAMPED for days. At times, things felt fine—but then the wrenching pain would return, low and sharp, curling her inward. Her bathroom visits were frequent and intense.

She wasn't alone.

Others on Nameth were sick too. Workers dragged themselves through shifts, weakened and dehydrated, trying to keep the schedule intact. Faces were pale. Buckets had been placed discreetly—in corners of the work hall, even out in the fields.

Bree stepped out into the grow yard. The gray light added to the gloom, casting the tiered shelving in dull metallic shadow. The racks held tight to their rows of leafy greens, uniform and silent. The air smelled faintly of plastic and algae.

She spotted Ian crouched near the lowest point in the irrigation system. He twisted a valve, draining a foul-smelling liquid into a catch bucket. Bree instinctively held her breath—it smelled like the bathroom she'd just left.

No one had said anything about the food being unsafe. No posted notice. No update on the board.

She wrapped her arms around her stomach and thought of Talem. There, they talked about everything.

Bad news was shared alongside good. People could ask questions. Make their own plans.

Bree made her way to the washroom near the back of the dormitory block. The door stuck slightly before giving way, hinges grating with a sound she felt in her teeth.

Inside, the light buzzed overhead—dim and flickering. She turned the faucet. Water came, but only just. Tepid. Not cold. Not hot.

She cupped a handful, splashed it on her face, then stared into the scratched metal mirror. Skin pale. Eyes tired. She wondered, briefly, if feeling better on the inside would make things look better out there.

There was no soap.

She stepped out into the corridor, still drying her hands on her pants, when she nearly ran into her father.

He was walking slowly, like he wasn't quite sure where he should go next. He paused when he saw her, jaw tightening a fraction before softening.

"Bree," he said. "You alright?"

"I'm fine," she lied.

He nodded, but didn't move on. For a moment, he just stood there, looking past her down the hallway. His eyes were red-rimmed. Tired.

"You headed to the grow yard?" she asked.

He shook his head. "Already been. Systems check came back normal."

Bree didn't answer. She didn't need to.

He cleared his throat and glanced down. "We're managing it. There's just... been some stress on the lines. Things'll settle down soon."

She nodded slowly. "If people knew what was going on, they'd probably be less afraid."

He gave a thin smile. "People don't need more fear, Bree. They need direction. One step, then another."

He started to move past her, then paused. "Get some rest," he said. "You don't look great."

Neither do you, she thought.

But she only said, "Thanks. I'll try."

That evening, she slipped into the radio room while the others were still finishing dinner. No one was really paying attention anymore—not to her, at least.

Lina wasn't on the channel.

But someone named Peter was. He listened as she spoke, quietly at first, telling him about the sickness going around. She hadn't meant to say much—but he was really listening. As if taking notes. As if her words mattered.

And then, before she could stop herself, it came out.

"They moved all the boats," she said. "I don't know where they are. But I know for sure—we can't go anywhere."

A pause. Then: "We're prisoners here."

On Talem, Peter sat alone in the radio room, notebook open, pencil hovering just above the page.

He'd expected a routine evening scan. Maybe a check-in from one of the outlying farms. Instead, he found himself leaning closer to the speaker, scribbling furiously as Bree's voice broke through—shaky at first, then suddenly clear.

The residents of Nameth were prisoners.

The words hung in the static.

Peter didn't respond right away. He didn't want to startle her. Instead, he flipped back a few pages in his notebook, double-checking his notes.

It was adding up.

He keyed the mic, voice steady. "Copy that, Bree. We hear you. Just stay on channel nine when you can. We'll keep listening."

Then he stood, tore the page from the pad, and started for Erik's door.

CHAPTER TWENTY-FOUR

IT HAD TAKEN THEM DAYS to collect the fuel. Plastic tubes snaked into almost-empty tanks—siphoning a little from here, a little from there. Now they had it. Five gallons. Just enough to get them to the island—and, if they were careful, back again.

Risky, heading out like this. But tough times called for desperate measures.

They were sure they'd find what they were looking for. The island had seals. Everyone knew that. What they didn't know was what else they'd find. The place stayed dark at night. Too far offshore to spot movement in daylight. Most likely there were people. But this wasn't a robbery.

At least, that's what they told themselves.

They weren't stealing. They were taking what was there—what was wild and free and, in their minds, just as much theirs as anyone's.

The sea was as calm as it ever was. Deep swells moved beneath them, rising and falling as though something breathed just below the surface. The outboard sputtered now and then, coughing through a drop in pressure before catching again. The men didn't speak. One held the red fuel can between his boots, shifting it every so often as if that might make it last longer. His right hand stayed steady on the tiller, steering the small boat into the low waves. The others held tight, fists clenched around the baseball bats they'd brought.

The island was close now. They spotted a farm—green fields clustered tight around a house, crops nearing harvest. The man on the rudder adjusted course, veering them away.

They weren't here for that.

They were headed around the north end, to the west side.

The wild side.

Kiernan looked up at the sound of a small engine, the noise rising and falling as it fought the swells. His eyes narrowed. A boat—low in the water—was creeping around the northern headland, just visible between breaks in the brush.

He dropped the long-bladed scythe he'd been using and turned for the house at a run.

This wasn't a visit. This was danger.

Kiernan burst through the porch door, boots thudding across the floor. He crossed the front room in three strides and keyed the mic hanging by the window.

"Channel Nine, this is Far North," he said, voice steady but clipped. "Got eyes on a small boat—single outboard, heading west around the point. Five aboard. Motor sounds rough. They're hugging the coast."

He let off the key, listening to static. Then pressed it again.

"I'd say they're headed around to the west side."

He held the mic. Still nothing.

Then: "Copy that, Far North. Stand by."

Sarah was already moving. She sprinted to the workshop, threw open the door. Erik and Callum looked up from their project.

"You need to hear this," she said, breath quick. "Sounds like we might have a different kind of visitor this time."

Erik didn't ask questions. He was out the door in seconds, Callum on his heels.

Back in the Radio Room, Sarah passed Erik the headset as he leaned in.

"Kiernan," Erik said, "what exactly are you seeing up there?"

A pause. Then Kiernan's voice came back—calm, focused.

"Hard to say. Five men. No gear I could see, but they're sitting stiff. Tense. Like they're not used to the boat. They cut wide past the farm—then turned toward the far side. Looks like they could be heading for Wren."

Erik looked up. Callum was clenching and unclenching his fists.

"Let's get Peter, Cari, Harald, and Lina," Erik said. "Bikes'll be fastest."

"I'll get them moving," Sarah said, already ducking out the door.

Erik keyed the mic again. "Kiernan, good catch. Cut west across the ridge, check in with Reid and Marla. Let them know what's coming—see if you can get eyes on the boat again."

"Already moving," Kiernan replied. "I'll be with them in thirty minutes, forty-five tops."

By the time Erik turned, Callum was already cinching his pack. Outside, bikes were coming off the hooks—wheels spinning, frames clattering onto gravel.

Peter arrived first, breathing hard. "I heard," he said simply.

Cari followed a moment later, face unreadable.

Then Lina and Harald, flushed from the sprint.

Erik raised a hand. "We don't know what this is yet. We approach calm, eyes open. If they've landed, we intercept. If they're still on the water, we track and call. Understood?"

Everyone nodded.

Erik hesitated, just a breath. Then: "Harald, grab the Theoben."

Kiernan moved fast through the thinning trees, boots crunching over damp needles, scythe long forgotten back at the field. The ridge curved above the western slope, a line he'd walked a hundred times—but never like this.

He crested a rise and dropped to one knee, scanning the coastline below.

There it was.

The boat had already pulled in—drawn up on a strip of sand just beyond the old boathouse. He squinted through the branches. The five men were onshore. Two dragged the bow higher up the beach. Another stood on the rocks, glancing out toward open water, then back around the cove.

They moved with purpose—but not haste.

One disappeared into the boathouse. The others slipped into the Wren outbuildings.

They'd gotten there faster than he expected.

Kiernan rose and started down the slope, loping through brush toward the Harrison farm. He'd grab Reid—and the Drifter boy—and meet Erik on the road.

"Nothing much in here," one of the men called up from the boathouse as the others passed. "Just some old sailboat." He stepped back out and jogged to catch up.

They'd already entered the outbuilding.

The air inside was stale, the floor tracked with dust and pine needles. A sagging workbench stood against the wall, cluttered with rusted tools. Nothing useful. Nothing worth their time.

They'd already spotted the seal colony down the coast. No need to rush—but no reason to linger either.

They were turning to leave when one of them paused. "Wait."

He stepped toward the back wall. Something was off—a section of boards slightly misaligned. Subtle. But not accidental.

His hand reached back into the dark cavity, fingers brushing wood, then curling around something cold and metallic. He gripped the curve of the barrel and gave it a tug.

"This might be worth the whole trip," he said, pulling the shotgun into the light.

He crouched again, reaching further.

"There's shells here too," he added, voice rising as a grin spread across his face.

One of the others let out a low whistle. Another shifted his grip on the bat and looked away.

"Careful with that," someone muttered.

But the man just ran his hand down the barrel, pleased. "It's clean," he said. "Somebody oiled it before stashing it."

No one answered. For a moment, the space held still— thick with dust and the quiet suggestion that something had just changed.

Reid and Mark were waiting when Kiernan arrived. Sarah had radioed ahead, and they'd met him at the edge of the farm.

"What do you think they want?" Reid asked. "I'm guessing you don't think this is a social call."

Kiernan's gaze moved from Reid to Mark. The old farmer was resolute. The young Drifter looked nervous—understandable, given what he'd already lived through.

"They were carrying bats," Kiernan said evenly. "I think they're headed for the seals. A raid. Grab and go."

Mark spoke up, unexpected but clear. "We have to stop this. It's not right."

"Come on," Reid said, nodding. "Let's get up the road. Better we meet Erik before he passes us."

They started walking toward the Wren property. Only as they moved did Kiernan notice the axe Reid was holding low at his side. He hoped it wouldn't come to that. But he also knew: Reid didn't like being messed with.

The men made their way back down to the boat, bats swinging loosely with each stride.

"Let's move the boat up to the seal colony," one man said. "We need it close. We'll kill as many as we can fit. Should hold at least eight."

They shoved the boat into the shallows. The motor coughed once, then caught on the second pull. Slowly, they guided it south—toward the pebble beach where the seals lay stretched in the sun, unaware.

Erik and the others from Talem had crested the last rise above the Wren shoreline, bikes left behind where the trail narrowed to footpath. Erik led, with Lina and Harald just behind, then Callum, Peter, and Cari moving quietly through the trees. The brush broke as they neared the overlook, and up ahead they spotted movement—three figures standing. Reid, Mark, and Kiernan at the tree line, already watching the cove.

Kiernan turned as they approached. "They moved the boat," he said, low and urgent. "It's down past the headland, by the seals."

They gathered at the edge of the bluff. From this angle, they could see the shallow crescent of beach, gray stones shimmering in the weak light. And the seals—dozens of them—speckled the shoreline, slick bodies sprawled across rock and sand.

The boat was beached again, engine ticking faintly as it cooled. The five men were climbing out, two of them already moving toward the animals. Bats in hand.

No one spoke.

Down below, a seal lifted its head at the sound of footsteps. Another shifted, tail twitching toward the sea.

And then it came—the sudden arc of a bat. A sharp *crack* echoed up the hillside.

One of the seals jerked, writhed.

Another blow.

Harald flinched.

Cari stepped forward, eyes locked on the scene unfolding below.

Another seal tried to drag itself toward the water, half-sliding over the rocks. A man moved quickly after it, raising his bat again.

Callum swore under his breath.

Erik's voice was hard and quiet. "This ends now."

They moved as one, boots crunching over the bluff trail, pushing down toward the beach. The men hadn't noticed them yet. Not until Erik called out.

"Hey!" he shouted, voice ringing across the cove. "That's enough."

The men turned. The one with the shotgun stepped forward slightly, wide stance in the sand. He tilted his head, almost amused.

"Who the hell are you?"

Erik didn't flinch. "Put the weapons down. Walk away."

The man laughed—a short, flat sound. "From what? Some village locals? These aren't *your* seals. They're food. We have the right to them. We'll take what we can carry."

Behind Erik, the Talem group held their ground. No one spoke.

Then, from beside Harald, Lina's voice cut the air.

"No!"

It cracked like a twig underfoot.

The man turned, slowly. "Have it your way."

202

And before anyone could move, he swung the shotgun—not at them, but down, toward a seal scrambling for the water. The blast tore through the silence. The seal bucked once, then collapsed, twitching on the stones. A splash of red hit the gray surf. Shards of bone, skin, and blubber scattered across the beach.

Time fractured.

Harald stared, frozen—Theoben in his left hand, not even raised.

Cari stepped forward. No hesitation.

"Give it," she whispered.

He let go.

She brought it to her shoulder in one smooth motion, feet planted, breath steady. The Theoben cracked—not loud, but sharp and final.

The man with the shotgun jerked, staggered.

Then dropped.

Sand puffed around him as he fell, the weapon tumbling from his hand.

Everyone stood, rooted in place.

The men among the seals.

Mark and Reid.

Cari.

She lowered the rifle. It slipped from her hands and thudded to the ground.

No one spoke.

It was Callum who moved first.

He walked past the others without a word, bent, and picked up the shotgun lying in the blood-streaked sand. The fallen man didn't move.

Callum turned toward the boat—half-beached on the stony shore—and raised the shotgun. One blast. The outboard engine cracked open, plastic and metal torn in an instant.

He stepped into the surf, cold water curling around his boots. Took the shotgun by the barrel. With a full-body swing, he hurled it far into the bay.

They watched it arc and disappear.

The silence didn't last.

One of the men dropped his bat. It clattered on the stones, sharp and sudden in the quiet.

Another stepped backward, eyes fixed on the body— on the red blooming beneath the fallen man's chest.

The one nearest the water turned toward the boat, saw the shattered casing of the motor, the fuel dripping into the surf. He let out a sound—not quite a word, more like a breath punched from his lungs.

"You killed him," one of them said, voice thin. Not angry. Just trying to make sense of what had happened.

Erik stepped forward slowly, hands still visible, voice low. "You brought weapons. You used them. You took what wasn't yours."

"No one owns seals," the tallest man said, but his voice had lost its weight. "We just—we needed something to trade. We're trying to stay alive."

"And now?" Callum said quietly, his boots still in the water.

None of the men answered.

Erik took a step forward, his voice steady. "Come with us. We'll figure out how this ends. You'll get your chance to speak—but the island will hear the whole story."

The men didn't move at first. Then slowly, one after another, they dropped their weapons—bats clattering to the stones, hands raised just enough to show they understood.

Harald bent to pick up the Theoben where Cari had let it fall. He wanted to look at her, to say something—but for some reason, he couldn't. His chest felt tight. The seal still lay bleeding in the surf.

Lina was already at Cari's side, whispering something low. Cari didn't answer, just kept her eyes on the man she'd dropped.

Above them, gulls circled wide and slow. The waves lapped the stones like nothing had changed.

CHAPTER TWENTY-FIVE

GRACE ARRIVED LATE IN THE AFTERNOON. The men were held securely in one of the farm's root cellars—provided with a simple meal courtesy of Marla. Sarah was standing by in the Radio Room back in town, surrounded by townspeople anxious to hear what had happened. It would be awkward, but she would transmit to the other farms what was said, and relay any comments.

Erik began: "Let's bring the meeting to order."

Grace kept the minutes. They would be entered into the library records, like all important meetings on Talem. Available to all who asked.

Sarah's voice came over the radio, "We've got a request to back up here. We want the full story—the facts. What happened?"

Erik touched Harald's elbow. "Harald, why don't you be in charge of the mic. Transmit what we say here."

Harald moved over to the radio, holding down to transmit. "Kiernan spotted a boat earlier today. It ran up around the top of the island and beached at the Wren property." He glanced back to Erik who nodded for him to continue. "There were five men on board. They landed close to the boathouse then went into the outbuildings. That's where they found a shotgun."

He stopped there. The people in the room knew this but it was likely news to Sarah's group and the other outlying farms who were listening in.

Sarah broke the uneasy silence of the room. "We have a question from the Gaithers. They want to know how there happened to be a shotgun at Wren. Haven't we been through all these buildings before?"

Harald looked up toward his father. "Let Sarah know that the shotgun was known to be kept there but it was hidden and presumed safe."

Harald relayed the message, feeling a hot flush start to touch his face. Actions had consequences. Just as inaction could have a consequence too.

There was a pause on the line.

Then Sarah again: "Understood. The Gaithers say thank you. No judgment—just looking for clarity."

"Harald, why don't you continue with the facts," Erik said. "Let's get everyone caught up, and maybe we save the questions until they've heard it all,"

Harald repeated Erik's request to hold questions and continued. "The men moved their boat next to the seal colony. When we arrived they had disembarked from the boat. They were walking among the seals." He paused momentarily, just to catch a breath. "They walked among them. They had baseball bats. By the time we were close enough to shout at least two of the seals had been killed."

The room was quiet as they relived the harrowing moments on the beach.

"My dad, Erik, called for them to stop. But the man with the shotgun got angry. He opened fire on a seal that was headed to the water. It was awful."

Callum cleared his throat and muttered, "Go on Harald, out with it."

"Cari took the Theoben," Harald continued. "She stopped him from killing any more. One shot." He tried to look over at her, but his gaze only made it as far as Lina whose eyes were full of tears. "After that Callum took the shotgun and shot through their motor, then he threw the gun into the sea. It's gone now."

There was no reply from the radio.

Then Sarah's voice again, softer now. "Heard and understood."

Peter stepped forward. "We need to decide what to do with the four that remain. That's why we're here."

Now it was Erik who spoke, "I think we should all have some time. Those who want to speak need an opportunity to be heard. Where do we think we are—what should we do."

Callum stood. "I think it's pretty clear what I think. These men, they cannot be allowed to leave. They'll go back to the mainland and next week there'll be ten men, not five." He looked around the room, challenging others to deny it. "We don't have clear rules here. No real leader.

It's a problem. How can people know how to act if you don't have rules?"

The question hung, then he looked over to Grace, "Don't you have one of your stories for this, Grace?"

She waited, a wry look flashed and was gone. "Callum, I'm afraid I don't have a story. In fact... this is the story. Where we go from here will determine who we are and what we are. It's up to us."

Harald forced himself to his feet. The mic was still in his hand and transmitting as he spoke. "I think we've already shown who we are."

Finally he was able to take his gaze as far as Cari. "You can't come to Talem and kill seals." Cari looked back matching the intensity on his face.

"You can't come to Talem to take. What we have here—we built it," he turned to Callum. "We might not have rules. Not written down. But we have morals, and we have ways we act. We need to be proud of who we are, and how we've acted here." His voice trailed off, like he'd said enough, even if he hadn't said it all.

There was a murmur in the room—low, thoughtful. Not agreement, not dissent. Just people breathing again.

Cari didn't look away from Harald. "I'm not sorry I pulled the trigger," she said. "But I didn't want to. I didn't want it to be me."

Grace gave a small nod, almost imperceptible.

Reid cleared his throat. "So. What now? Four men in the cellar. Do we feed them for a season? Wait for another boat?"

Kiernan spoke from the doorway. "We could set them ashore on Kingsley. Give them some supplies. Let them cool their heels."

Callum frowned. "Send them to the Gulag?"

Lina stepped forward, quiet but sure. "Maybe it's not about what they deserve. Maybe it's about what we can live with."

"I think Lina has struck something here," Grace said. "But I think we have another step. We are acting as judge and jury. I think it might be time to let the defendants have a moment."

There was a quiet rustle as people shifted in their seats. No one rushed to agree, but no one objected either.

"They're in the cellar," Reid said. "I can bring them up. One at a time, or all together."

Erik looked around the room, weighing. "Together," he said finally. "Let them see us. Let them speak to the people who were there."

Kiernan stepped out with Reid. A few moments later, the four remaining men were led into the meeting space. Their clothes were still salt-marked from the surf. None of them looked defiant. One kept his eyes on the floor. Another scanned the room like he was still trying to gauge whether this was a trap.

"You have a chance to speak," Erik said. "Say what you need to say. No one will interrupt."

The man who had dropped his bat on the beach—the youngest—stepped forward. He looked exhausted. His voice was raw.

"We didn't come here to steal anything," he said. "We didn't even want to kill. We came to survive."

The others were nodding and another spoke up, "I've got a family, a kid. We're starving on the mainland. It's not like here."

Finally, one of the men who'd been silent till now murmured, "We're sorry. We didn't know if there were people here. We didn't know that you cared."

There was a stillness after his words—long enough that the wind outside could be heard brushing through the orchard.

Erik's gaze moved slowly across the room. "You didn't know if there were people here," he said. "But you came with bats. You used a gun."

The man who had spoken last didn't defend himself. Just nodded once, slow.

Reid folded his arms. "You thought this place was abandoned. That made it okay to kill?"

"No," the younger one said quickly. "But it made it easier to tell ourselves it was."

Grace looked down at her notes, then back up. "We all tell ourselves stories to make things easier," she said. "But stories don't always line up with the truth."

Cari hadn't moved. She spoke softly now, but every word landed clear. "I don't want to carry this. I will. But I don't want to. Don't pretend we had a choice—and you didn't."

Silence again.

Then Lina: "We still have to decide what we can live with."

"I think," Mark was half standing, half sitting, not sure if he had a place in this. "I think that all of our actions have consequences. You can try to avoid them. Pretend they don't exist. But that's wrong. They do exist and you will find that out sooner or later." He fell back into his seat, coloring at the neck, but Loretta leaned into him, a hand on his arm.

No one spoke for a long moment.

Then Erik looked toward the radio. "Sarah, are you still with us?"

Her voice came back steady. "We're here. All of us. The Gaithers say thank you—for letting it be... real."

Grace set down her pencil. "Maybe that's where we are now. Past the facts. Past the outrage. Sitting with what's real. What we do next doesn't need to be perfect. But it should be human."

Kiernan spoke from the back of the room. "We can't keep them locked up. And we can't pretend it didn't happen."

Reid gave a low grunt of agreement. "They need to leave. Or maybe they need to stay. But not because the option to leave was taken away, because they choose it. Choose to contribute.

Callum shook his head slightly but didn't argue.

Grace pondered it. A choice not a sentence. A different way. A better way? Maybe just leave it at different for now.

Erik looked around the room. "Alright then. Tomorrow, we decide what that looks like. For tonight— they stay in the cellar. Fed. Safe. And we sleep on what it means to be us."

There was no vote. Just a quiet murmur of assent. Not perfect. But Talem all the same.

Chapter Twenty-Six

THE FOUR MEN spent a long night in the chilly root cellar.

The people of Talem had come to a decision. They kept circling back to something Harald had said: *We have ways we act.*

Well, the men would see how people acted here—and maybe, just maybe, it would leave a mark.

They walked together to the beach at the south end of Wren Cove.

The seals were gone. Harald hoped not forever.

All that remained were four bodies.

Two seals that might have been sleeping. One man, still lying where he'd fallen. And the last seal—blown to pieces.

The men grimaced alongside the islanders at the brutal scene.

Callum, practical as ever, got things moving. "First the man."

They dug a hole back from the waterline. Deep enough.

And the man who had come to Talem to take was laid to rest—without ceremony, without a marker.

The ebb tide worked with Kiernan and one of the men as they dragged the mutilated seal through the low surf.

They walked deep enough that when it was released, it would keep going.

An offering to the gods, Harald thought. *Or perhaps to the orcas.*

Erik unsheathed two knives. He handed one to a man and pointed to one of the remaining seals.

"Nothing goes to waste here," he said.

The man nodded slowly, understanding now what was expected of him.

He and Erik would butcher the seals.

The rest of the day was spent walking the island, delivering meat to the farms.

They separated the outsiders, each man accompanied by two islanders.

Kiernan and Peter took one. Harald and Erik another. Callum and Cari a third.

Finally, Mark and Reid.

For a small island, the walks felt long. The sun was hot.

At each farm, the men were introduced—met with nods, silences, or small talk.

Varying degrees of warmth. But no doors were closed.

They reached the Harrison farm just as the sun tilted past its highest point. The fields shimmered with heat, and the goats watched from their shaded lean-to, chewing slowly, unconcerned.

Marla opened the door before they could knock. She saw the seal meat in Harald's pack, the man walking beside them, and the weary look on Erik's face. She didn't ask anything.

"Well," she said, stepping aside, "if you've come to trade, we've got sorrel and turnips. Might even have a few eggs."

Harald smiled faintly. "No trade today, Marla. Just delivery."

He passed her the bundle, carefully wrapped in waxed cloth. The man beside them—tall, grey-bearded, with nervous hands—shifted awkwardly.

Marla met his eyes. "You know how to cure meat?"

The man shook his head. "Not really."

"You'll learn," she said. "Everyone does."

She turned and disappeared into the kitchen. No invitation inside. But no rejection either.

As they turned to go, the man glanced back. "She didn't even ask my name."

Erik adjusted the strap on his shoulder. "She will. When it matters."

The path to the Jake's place was dry and narrow, lined with brittle grass and thistle. No one had mowed in weeks. When they crested the last rise, they saw Ruth Jakes waiting, arms folded, lips thin. Her husband wasn't visible, but the shed door was open—he was likely inside, listening.

Callum gave a short nod. Cari said nothing.

The man walking with them had tried once or twice to speak on the trail, but neither of them had answered. Now, standing in front of Ruth, he seemed to shrink a little.

"We brought meat," Callum said. He kept it flat, almost bored.

Ruth didn't move. "From those seals?"

"Yes," Cari said. "The ones your dog used to bark at."

That earned a twitch from Ruth's mouth, not quite a smile.

Cari unshouldered her pack and held out the wrapped parcel. Ruth didn't take it immediately. She looked at the man.

"And this one?" she asked.

"He's part of the work detail," Callum said. "For now."

Ruth's eyes stayed fixed. "He got a name?"

The man cleared his throat. "Colin."

"You from the mainland, Colin?"

"Yes, ma'am."

"You know how to build a fence?"

"A little."

Ruth finally reached out and took the meat. "Then tomorrow, you come back. We need one mended."

She turned and walked back toward the house. The door stayed open behind her, but no one invited them in.

They stood for a moment in the silence.

"Better than I expected," Colin muttered.

Callum gave a grunt. "You'll learn that on Talem, better than expected is as good as it gets."

Reid walked steadily, pack slung over one shoulder. Mark kept close, his companion—a lean, sun-dark figure who hadn't said a word since leaving the beach.

No one had asked him to speak.

They'd dropped off seal meat at the Gaither place. It was received with a thank you. The man had remained silent but his face showed a sorrow no one could miss.

The Fletcher place came into view slowly, not because it was far off the road, but because it was hard to see. Trees pressed close. Alder limbs arched over what had once been a front gate. The house was sagging in on itself, roof collapsed at the back corner. A wheelbarrow lay overturned, buried in thistle and pine needles.

Reid stopped. "Used to be a good place. There's a spring up the hill. Orchards still try to bloom in spring."

Mark stepped forward, brushing a branch aside. "We've talked about bringing it back. A team might do it over time."

The man finally spoke. "I might be able to help with that."

"Yes," Reid said. "You might."

The man looked around. "My name's Paul."

Mark nodded. "Come on Paul. Let's head back."

The sun was slanting low as they gathered again at the Harrison's. Marla and Lina had laid out tea—steaming mugs, a dish of dried apples, the comfort of something ordinary.

Grace welcomed each group with quiet thanks, but her eyes kept drifting to one person.

She pulled her aside. "I seem to remember that I owe you a book recommendation." Grace removed a small volume out of her grey weathered backpack.

Cari looked hard at the book, a hardcover that fit neatly in the palm of Grace's hand. "Heart of Darkness," she read aloud. "By Joseph Conrad."

"It's not an easy read," Grace said. "But it speaks to a darkness that follows us. Sometimes you have to be able to see that, so that you know when to take a step the other way."

Cari turned it over once in her hands. She didn't smile. But she didn't hand it back either.

Grace gave a small nod, then turned toward the others.

Inside the house, chairs had been pulled into a loose circle.

Erik stood by the hearth. He didn't raise his voice.

"We've talked among ourselves," he began, watching each of the men. "We live a certain way here on the island. We don't live in absolutes." He let the words settle.

"You've seen that today," he continued. "We will offer you a choice. The boat you came in still has oars. You can take it and row back to the mainland. Not easy—but not impossible."

The men exchanged glances, uncertain. Hoping for something else.

"Or... you can stay."

Erik's gaze moved from one face to the next.

"And if we stay," Paul spoke, low and anxious. "Will we ever be trusted?"

Grace answered carefully, "There's an old adage. You take people as you find them. Paul, I think that will be up to you."

"That's right," Erik said. "We have places that need care. Neighbors who need help. You can work with us, live among us—become part of what we are. But you'll have to believe in it. That's the only way it works."

CHAPTER TWENTY-SEVEN

HARALD ARRIVED AT THE WORKSHOP EARLY. The Theoben was cleaned and back in the locked cabinet before anyone else showed up. He spent the next couple of hours tinkering—projects long ignored, half-finished things. But only part of him was paying attention.

By mid-morning, when she still hadn't shown up, he packed up his tools and left. He'd find Lina. She'd know.

His first stop was the greenhouses. No sign of her.

He wandered a while, head down, a fog hanging over him he couldn't seem to shake.

At the clinic, he finally found her—deep in conversation with Jana and Hamish. A spread of texts lay open between them. Hamish was scribbling furiously.

Lina looked up at the sound of his boots on the floor. "Cari's not here," she said. "I don't think she wants to be found right now... but you could try the library."

He muttered his thanks and turned back down the path.

He wasn't sure why he hadn't thought of the library in the first place.

He was halfway there before his pace began to slow.

Maybe it would be better to leave her be.

Let time do its work.

He wasn't sure she'd even want to talk—to *him*, of all people.

Harald entered cautiously. The front stacks hid most of the space from view.

A few steps in, he could see their usual spot by the high south window—but it was empty.

He was starting to think she didn't want to be found.

Then he saw her.

Cari was half-sunk into one of the kids' beanbags, a book in hand.

She looked up, met his gaze.

It wasn't an invitation—but it didn't say *go away*, either.

He approached slowly, dragged one of the beanbags from the corner, and sank down beside her on the library floor.

Cari didn't speak.

He waited.

Their quiet breathing was the only sound in the room.

Then, finally, the words he'd been carrying for days came loose.

"I'm sorry," he said. "It should've been me. I was the one holding the gun. I could've taken the shot...

"I wish it *had* been me."

She looked at him and then back to the book held tightly in her lap.

"Did you know they used to kill elephants for their tusks?" she said. Her voice was low, flat. "Just left the rest to rot."

"I know they used to kill whales," he said, matching her tone. "Just for the oil. They'd throw the carcasses back into the sea."

She flipped a page, searching for something. Found it.

Read aloud: "'It was unearthly, and the men were—no, they were not inhuman. Well, you know that was the worst of it—the suspicion of their not being inhuman.'"

She looked at him.

"Harald... what if this thing inside us—inside *me*—what if it wants to come out again?"

He sat with that a moment.

"What you did... that wasn't the darkness," he said quietly. "The darkness was in *them*. In the man who pulled the trigger on a helpless creature."

The words hung between them.

"You're the one who stopped it," he went on. "Stopped it when no one else could. Not me. Not Erik. Not even Callum. It was you."

Cari didn't answer.

But she reached for him—took his hand in both of hers.

And then the tears came.

They held on tightly, both crying now. Crying and gripping each other as if the ground might give way.

Eventually, the tears slowed. Not gone entirely—just rain easing after a long storm.

"Something's going on at the clinic," he said softly. "Lina's there. Will you come? See what they're working on?"

Cari nodded, not trusting her voice. She wiped her eyes with the sleeve of her sweatshirt, then stood with him. The room felt changed—like something coming back into focus.

When they reached the clinic, they found the door propped open, voices drifting from inside—low and focused.

Lina was bent over the big table with Jana and Hamish, papers spread wide.

Cari and Harald paused at the doorway, but Lina looked up and waved them in. "You should see this," she said. "We think we've got something."

Cari and Harald stepped closer to the table. Papers were spread in uneven layers—some scribbled with notes, others marked with rough pencil diagrams. There were cross-sections of what looked like trenches, outlines of simple structures, and lists of ingredients. An old field medic's manual lay open, its spine cracked, corners curled from years of use.

Lina moved aside as Jana stepped forward, one hand resting lightly on the table.

"Grace originally asked me to document Nameth's systems," she said. "For the archive. But once I started looking into them, I couldn't stop. The systems are breaking down—not just because of age, but because they were never meant to serve so many people. It's too dense. Too centralized. And now with the sickness…"

She trailed off for a moment, then picked up one of the sketches.

"So we shifted focus. Tried to think like first responders. What can you do fast, with what you already have?"

She pointed to a cross-section of a trench filled with layered materials.

"This is a basic filtration bed. If they can reroute their graywater—kitchen runoff, bathing water—into a trench like this, lined with gravel, sand, and biochar, it won't make the water drinkable, but it should reduce the bacterial load before it reaches the outflow."

Hamish spoke from behind her. "Charcoal's the key. It binds pathogens and parasites. We've got enough here to send some. If we burn slow and cool, we can make more."

Jana nodded. "We're also including a vinegar wash. Not industrial—just fermented. You take fruit, a little honey if they've got it, and wild yeast. In a week or two, it's a mild disinfectant. Not perfect, but better than rinsing with plain water."

Cari leaned over the table, scanning the lines and notes. "And this helps *us*, too?"

Lina stepped in. "That's the other part. We think the outflow on their side can be buffered. Right now it empties straight into the channel. But if they stack rock and sand at the mouth—build a break line—and plant reed beds around the edge, it slows the spread. Gives time for the natural bacteria to break things down before it reaches open water."

"It's not a fix," Jana said. "But it's something. If they're willing to try it."

There was a quiet pause. Just the sound of the wind pressing gently at the clinic walls.

Harald looked down at the papers, then up at the others.
"I think we should send it," he said. "Whether they use it or not... it's the right thing to do."

They headed over to the radio room, where Sarah was at the desk. She looked up as they heaved open the stubborn door.

"We need to reach out to Nameth," Jana said, holding up a folded packet of notes and drawings. "Can you call? I need to speak to Ian or Clare... if they're willing to listen."

"Hang on," Sarah said, adjusting the gain as she turned the dial. The faint murmur of static gave way to a sharper signal—Channel 9.

"This is Talem Station," she said into the mic. "We have documentation for the attention of Ian or Clare on your side. Do you copy?"

The reply came back after a pause. "Stand by, Talem."

It took some time to find Clare and Ian, but eventually both came on the line—ready to listen.

Jana leaned in and took the mic. "We have a series of mitigation plans related to the recent illness. We know this wasn't requested. But we're offering them freely."

Clare's voice came through, faint but steady. "Thank you, Talem Station. We'll receive the transmission. Ian will copy down all suggestions. We'll see what we can do."

Erik had heard about the activity in Comms and stepped quietly into the room just as Jana was finishing with the information. He motioned to Sarah, who nodded and handed him the mic.

"Clare, this is Erik," he said. "Let us know if you need help with any of it. We have people—and at least some know how. We're ready, if you want us."

There was a pause on the other end.

"Thank you, Erik," Clare said at last. "We'll talk about it. I... appreciate the help. Nameth out."

Sarah pushed her chair back from the desk.

"I guess we'll see where that lands," she said. "But at least this time, they listened."

The others moved toward the door.

Harald and Cari stayed close, walking as one.

Lina murmured something to Jana, and Hamish gathered the notes under one arm and headed back toward the clinic.

Bree sat down to lunch with Sammy. They weren't serving food from the racks anymore—only what was growing in the fields below the farm.

She looked at the potato on her plate and nudged it with her fork, as if it might turn into something more interesting. Her stomach still griped, but she took a few bites—just enough to get through the afternoon.

Afterward, they walked together as far as the center path. Sammy veered off toward her assignment, waving as she went.

"I'll see you at dinner, Bree."

Bree gave a nod but said nothing.

She wasn't sure she'd make it to dinner.

When she reached the greenhouse, she didn't stop. She kept walking—past the rows of lettuce and beans, past the toolshed and the boundary stakes, past the far edge of the compound.

Up.

Away from the commune.

Past the headland, over the ridge, and down toward the next bay.

CHAPTER TWENTY-EIGHT

MARK LIFTED THE T-POST DRIVER and let it fall under its own weight—adding just enough push to drive the metal deeper into the soil.

They'd be doing this all day.

He'd learned to pace himself. Burning out before lunch didn't do anyone any good.

Loretta was working with Reid a little farther down the line, stringing wire between the posts. Mark didn't know where the old man got his energy, but they were expanding the pasture—getting it ready for the new goats expected in the spring.

He paused and lifted his gaze, taking in the land as it gave way to water.

This was where the island changed.

The soft beaches of the east coast gave way to the rougher edge of the west—but here, along the north side, was something else.

A kind of quiet beauty. A meeting place between forest and field, between pasture and the sea.

Just three miles across the strait, he could see Nameth—its shape a mirror of the land they worked.

Coastline and farmland giving way to trees, then to wildness.

Mark dropped his gaze, turning back to the work. Reid understood the beauty of this place more than anyone, but you didn't have all day to stand and stare in his world.

Bree kept to the brushline until the last slope gave way to the bay.

She made her way down toward the house—it was still there, barely. The roof had collapsed, and vines had claimed most of the southern wall. But beyond it, the old boathouse looked intact.

She wasn't sure why she didn't just keep going. There could be another place farther along, better sheltered, better kept.

But something in her pulled toward the boathouse.

The side door swung open easily, as if the hinges had been oiled not long ago. The floor was clear of debris. A broom stood in the corner.

And on the lift sat a white motorboat—the same one they'd once used to visit Talem.

So this is where they'd gone. The harbor boats, hidden away. Not scrapped, not destroyed—just moved. Out of harm's way.

Out of temptation.

She drew a breath.

It felt right.

Almost like the boat had been waiting for her here, all along.

She lowered the boat into the water.

The handle was stiff and the lift groaned, lowering the hull with a hollow slap. The motorboat rocked in the shallows, nosing gently against the dock. She climbed in—unsteady for a moment—then found her footing.

The fuel gauge hovered just above empty. Barely enough to move the needle.

She stared at it for a long second.

Then turned the key.

The engine coughed once. Twice. Then caught.

She didn't smile. Didn't hope.

She gripped the wheel and eased it into reverse, backing out of the boathouse. The water spun the bow gently, turning her toward open sea.

There wasn't time to think.

The boat had been waiting. It felt right.

She slipped it out of neutral and gave it throttle.

Pointed the bow south.

South to Talem.

Mark was halfway through his next post when he heard it—a low mechanical thrum, faint but distinct against the usual rhythm of gulls and wind.

He paused, straightened, and scanned the horizon.

There. A boat. White hull. Moving slow and uncertain across the strait, maybe three-quarters of a mile offshore. It was underway but wrong, somehow. Listing just slightly in the water, too near to idle.

He dropped the post driver and stepped forward for a better view.

The engine sputtered once. Then again.

Then silence.

The boat rocked in place, the bow drifting as the current took hold.

For a moment nothing happened.

Then a figure climbed onto the gunwale and dove—clean and sudden—into the water.

Mark blinked.

Whoever it was didn't hesitate. Just started swimming. Strong strokes. No life vest. No pack.

He turned sharply. "Loretta!" he called. "Reid! There's someone in the water—offshore!"

They came quickly, Loretta wiping her hands on her jeans, Reid already moving fast.

"Where?" Reid asked.

Mark pointed. "About a mile out. From the boat—just went in. Headed this way."

Reid squinted. "Damn fool move," he muttered. "But it's a straight shot. Let's go."

They started down the slope toward the beach, boots crushing the dry grass, sun flashing low on the water.

Behind them, the boat bobbed aimlessly, slowly drifting north or west.

By the time they reached the shore, the swimmer was close.

Her strokes had slowed. Each one deliberate, heavy. Her head dipped below the surface once, then surfaced again—arms still churning through the last reach of open water.

Mark kicked off his boots and waded in.

The water was colder than he expected. Sharp around his knees, then thighs. He pushed forward until he could reach her.

"Got you," he said, more to himself than to the girl.

Bree didn't stop swimming. But when his hand found her shoulder, she let it rest there—for a moment.

Then her feet touched bottom and she staggered forward under her own weight, gasping, eyes fixed on the shore.

Loretta was waiting. She had a sweater in her hands and offered it up without a word.

Reid had already started a small fire with driftwood— the lighter flicking once, then catching.

No one asked who she was.

They knew.

Bree dropped to her knees at the edge of the tide line, doubled over, coughing hard. Then she sat back, stripped off her soaked shirt, and pulled on Loretta's sweater, still shivering.

Mark crouched beside her. "You made it," he said quietly.

Bree looked at him—eyes rimmed red, but steady.

"Yeah," she said. "Barely."

CHAPTER TWENTY-NINE

THE GREY SKY FELT LOW, like it could touch the ground at any moment.

Overcast in shifting tones of slate and shadow, the wind tore in off the sea—a biting draft that spoke of winter.

Winter, any day now.

Harald and Mark worked side by side.

Their axes rose and fell, splitting dry logs cleanly.

The rhythm was steady, unhurried—marked more by companionship than urgency.

The boys paused, letting Lisa catch up.

She was stacking handcarts for delivery—bundles of wood headed to homes around town.

Harald thought she was doing an outstanding job. She worked steadily, carefully, and—unlike his sister—left aside any insightful but uninvited commentary.

"It's going to be great having you in town this winter," he said. "I still can't believe Reid agreed to it."

"Yeah," Mark said, resting the axe across his shoulder. "Once we figured out we could pen the goats near town and feed them from down here, he kinda gave up the fight."

Harald smiled, trying to picture Reid backing down.

"We opened up one of the abandoned houses on the edge of town," Mark went on. He was grinning now. "You're not going to believe this—I've got my own room. The girls all decided to share a room. Even Bree. Apparently, after sleeping in a dorm all that time, she actually likes sharing."

"Marla must be in heaven with three girls around. You can give me the tour tonight," Harald said, setting the axe upright again. "Dinner at your place. I've planned a special dish. Hope you're ready."

The wind carried woodsmoke from hearths all across town, the scent curling through the streets.

Inside the radio room, Loretta and Sarah sat side by side.

"He never let me touch it," Loretta said, eyeing the shortwave. "Not once. Like I'd break it just by looking."

Sarah laughed, shaking her head as she guided Loretta's hand to the dial.

"Shortwave sets are tougher than people think," she said. "And you've got a steady hand. Go ahead—ease it back half a notch."

Loretta turned the dial, brow furrowed, but her hand was smooth and sure. Static gave way to a faint, distant signal—just a few scattered words riding the noise.

"I could've done this years ago," she muttered, but she was smiling now. "He just didn't want to admit I was better at it."

Sarah leaned back. "Well, now you'll know when he's bluffing."

"We're in town till spring," Loretta said. "I'd like to help here sometimes, if that's alright."

"It's more than alright," Sarah said. "You'd be surprised how few people volunteer."

Loretta nudged the dial again, carefully. "I wonder if there's anyone out there like us," she said. "If there are, I'd like to talk to them."

The clinic smelled of dried herbs and something vaguely antiseptic—potato alcohol.

Lina could see the small still in the corner, dripping its potent liquid into a jar. She wondered if Callum might be coming later to share a taste with Hamish, even though it was supposed to be strictly medicinal.

She was perched on a stool beside the long wooden cabinet, reading handwritten labels aloud as Hamish squinted into a tray of dark glass bottles.

"Comfrey. Arnica. This one's... maybe elderberry?"

Hamish leaned in. "That's elderberry, alright. The handwriting's harder to read every year, but the color's right."

Lina set it aside in the "still usable" box and reached for the next jar. "I should start a new labeling system. You can't fix the old world's handwriting."

Hamish gave a half-laugh. "You sure you're not ten years older than you say?"

"I'm just efficient," she said, deadpan.

He sat back with a sigh and wiped his hands on a cloth. "You should take a break. Go help with the dinner. I heard there's something special planned."

"I will," Lina said, without looking up. "But first I need to drop something at Grace's."

Hamish didn't ask what. He just nodded and turned back to his bottles.

The wind was biting harder by the time Lina reached Grace's porch.

She knocked once, then stepped inside without waiting. Grace was there at the table, a blanket over her lap and a cup of tea steaming by her elbow. The stove warmed the kitchen, but didn't quite reach as far as the table.

Lina pulled a folded paper from her coat and set it gently beside the cup.

"I copied your rabbit story," she said. "It was buried in that notebook that was barely holding together. I didn't think anyone else would be able to read it."

Grace looked at the paper, then at her. "That wasn't meant for anyone but me."

"I know," Lina said. "But now it is."

Grace smiled, not wide, but genuine. "You think it's time?"

Lina nodded. "I do."

Grace reached for the story, running a thumb along the edge of the paper. She handed it back to Lina, "Why don't you hang on to it until tonight. We can tell it together."

The smell of wild garlic hit them as soon as they stepped inside.

Harald glanced at Lina, who raised an eyebrow. "She started without you."

In the kitchen, Cari had the old cookbook open to the pasta page, a dusting of flour already across the counter. The pasta maker stood on the table, clamped into place, its roller gleaming faintly in the late light.

Harald kicked off his boots. "I was hoping you'd wait."

Cari didn't look up. "As usual, you're going to have to catch up."

Lina dropped her coat on the peg and moved to wash her hands. "You seem to make a habit out of schooling my brother. I think you might be my hero."

"Come on, I've barely started," Cari said, turning the page with the back of her wrist. "It seems pretty straightforward—but that roller thing scares me."

Harald stepped beside her, scooped out a well of flour on the board, and cracked in two eggs. The yolks slumped like little suns in the middle.

They got to work.

It was slow, uneven—flour too dry at first, then too wet. But before long, the dough came together. They kneaded it in turns, palms pressing and folding, until it felt right—elastic and smooth.

Cari fed the first sheet through the roller. Harald caught it on the other side. Lina followed with a dusting of flour to keep it from sticking.

It wasn't textbook. A little lopsided. A tear here and there. Perfect.

The room filled with the warmth of movement, of hands working in rhythm.

No one talked much. They didn't need to.

When the pasta was cut and drying, they began assembling the rest: a pot of stewed tomatoes, goat butter warmed with garlic and crushed herbs, a pan of crumbled goat cheese set aside to top each dish before serving.

By the time they finished, the kitchen smelled like something from an older time.

A handcrafted memory.

When the plates were empty and the forks set down, firelight flickered across a wall, and the guests settled back—relaxing in the afterglow of the shared meal.

Callum leaned back in his chair, rubbing his stomach. "That was... unreasonably good," he said. "Thank you, Marla. That sauce should be illegal."

Marla waved a hand. "You can thank Cari and Harald for the sauce. I want the recipe."

The room held that quiet fullness that followed a meal well earned. Chairs creaked. Someone stifled a yawn. Lisa had curled up against Loretta's side, already drifting.

Reid stood slowly, stretching. "Let's get that kettle going," he said. "We've still got a fire, and I think Grace has a story."

Heads turned toward Grace. She was near the hearth, eyes reflecting the flames.

She nodded once. "It's from another time," she said. "It's Lina's choice tonight."

Lina stood and crossed the room. From her coat, she pulled the folded paper and handed it to Grace. "You'll want this."

Grace took it without surprise, as if she'd been waiting.

And the room hushed.

Grace took the folded page and turned it once in her hands.

"I came across this one a long time ago," she said. "Didn't think I'd ever read it aloud."

She looked to Lina, who nodded.

"There was once a man who missed his home. An old country—still there, but out of reach."

Lina picked up the thread, "So he brought rabbits. Exactly twenty-four of them. A way to remember something from before." She looked at the room expectantly. "There weren't rabbits in the new country."

Grace resumed. "He turned them loose on the estate. The land was wide and the seasons gentle. And the rabbits did what rabbits do."

"There weren't any predators," Lina said. "No foxes, no wolves. No one was watching."

"Within a few seasons," Grace went on. "They weren't just his rabbits anymore. They ate the crops, then the grasses, and then the roots."

"They ruined the land," Lina shifted in her chair. "Before long there were thousands of them. Hundreds of thousands."

"It's true," Grace said. "They turned something balanced into something broken. The man died before he even saw what happened. But the people moved on. They adjusted, sometimes they fought them and sometimes they didn't. The rabbits are still there... but so are the people."

Lina smiled, happy she had a part in the story. "It's kind of about consequences. What happens when you don't think things through." She paused, and Erik got up and threw another log on the fire.

Luckily," she said. "We watch where we're stepping now."

The next day, Harald found himself drawn to Highpoint. The air was sharp with the edge of winter as he climbed at a slow, steady pace. No check-ins today—they could handle those from the radio room now.

Halfway up, he paused and looked back toward the harbor. He remembered the last ferry, the people who had left. Everything had changed after that day.

At the summit, he settled on the edge of an outcrop, knees drawn up. A bald eagle circled overhead, drifting on a current he couldn't see. Harald watched it for a while, then let his gaze sweep outward.

He thought about the four men. Three had chosen to stay. They were working the Fletcher place now, bringing it back from ruin—the ground cleared, rows marked, ready for potatoes come spring.

The late fall air was crisp and clear. For the first time in weeks, the mainland was more than a smudge. The smoke was gone. The fires had quieted. He wondered if they'd ever be connected again—if ferries might one day cross the channel to Talem.

Maybe someday, he would go. Not just to see what was left, but to find out what hope remained.

Below him, the wind stirred the trees. The island stood—battered, but breathing. The world had cracked, but the earth endured.

He rose and turned for the trail. Cari and Lina were cooking tonight. Harald was hoping for pasta.

Follow Timothy Hargreaves

Facebook:
@timothyhargreavesbooks

Goodreads:
https://www.goodreads.com/author/show/58453207.

www.timothyhargreaves.com

www.ingramcontent.com/pod-product-compliance
Lightning Source LLC
Chambersburg PA
CBHW022108240626
47153CB00007B/2276